I N 1945, **Milton Reynolds** introduced the ballpoint to the United States and triggered the biggest single-day shopping riot in history at Gimbels in Manhattan. The Reynolds International Pen Company made $5 million in eight weeks during the first non-wartime Christmas season. Thereafter, increasing competition from established companies such as Eversharp triggered several years of the "Pen Wars."

An exuberant entrepreneur who had already made and lost several fortunes, Reynolds bragged that he "stole it fair and square." This novel is told from his mild-mannered son Jim's point of view, about coping with Milton's outrageous schemes, then their sudden success.

More praise for *Mr. Ballpoint*:

"Puts *American Hustle* to shame. Jones has a marked talent for laying a methodical patina of logic over the most outlandish characters and events in his Rollo Hemphill novels. With *Mr. Ballpoint* he has turned that estimable gift to the true story of the wild entrepreneur Milton Reynolds who hustled his way to millions with the lowly ballpoint pen in the late 1940s. Reynolds lived the full, exciting "life of a salesman," and his outlandish career proves that truth can bat fiction out of the park any day."

Thomas Page, author of *The Man Who Wouldn't Die* and *The Hephaestus Plague*

"It's getting rarer these days to find humorous fiction—much less humor stories based on true stories—but Mr. Ballpoint is such a find and includes an unusual focus on a father-son relationship and a ballpoint pen. Not just for comedy readers and not just for those who want serious psychology... a recommendation for any who want a blend of entertainment and serious reading."

Diane Donovan, Senior Reviewer, Midwest Book Reviews and host of Donovan's Bookshelf

"Another important read coming from Gerald Everett Jones. He weaves together history, business acumen, science, and engineering, as well as the human condition, to produce a compelling story of America when capitalism still worked."

Jim Anton, author of *Santa Is Make-Believe, Isn't He?*

"Gerald Everett Jones sews a mast sail of a story that tackles the ever shifting winds of the development of first ballpoint pen, and the business knots that present themselves at every gale, charting a course towards a holiday sales rush that anchors every character in the book into the blustery capitalism that defines the American Dream of progress, and a brighter future for all."

Greg Minuskin, pen professional and member of Pen Collectors of America and Los Angeles Pen Club

"A fantastically entertaining read. I've always been fascinated by the history of the ordinary. Now every time I pick up a ballpoint pen I'll think of this story."

Nancy Shiffrin, author of *The Vast Unknowing* and *Games with Variations*

"Gerald Everett Jones tells the story in a way that brings back the fascination of the public [for an] event that parallels the frenzy of the introduction of the cellphone today—the pen that wrote without refilling, upside down, and under water. History more fascinating than fiction!"

Henry Gostony, coauthor of *The Incredible Ball Point Pen*

"Thank you, thank you, Gerald Everett Jones, for showing us that history can be hilarious and needn't involve King this or Queen that to be significant. Oh, and just so you know, I'm writing this endorsement with my turquoise Bic Velocity with the medium tip, which might not exist if not for Milt and Jim Reynolds. Love your writer's voice, BTW, Gerald! Keep those great books coming!"

Paula Berinstein, former producer and host, The Writing Show

"Milt always said, if you want to do the impossible you have to do it right away. It's amazing how many impossible things he achieved."

Mandy Boesche, granddaughter of Edna and Milton, daughter of Zelta and James Reynolds

"Understand that Milton Reynolds was not an immoral man. But you could say that he was an amoral man. Now, Jim Reynolds? He was as honest as they come. If you saw Gary Cooper as Longfellow Deeds, you get the idea. Oh, and I'm proud to say I'm the talented baby who appears near the end of this story."

Jessie Reynolds Groothius, MD,
granddaughter of Edna and Milton,
daughter of Zelta and James Reynolds

"Although truth is stranger than fiction, Gerald Everett Jones gets darn close to capturing the ebullient essence of Milton Reynolds in this highflying yarn about our granddad, from whom four generations have inherited their spirited, indefatigable, entrepreneurial genes."

Paula Golden, granddaughter of Edna and
Milton, daughter of Zelta and James Reynolds

"My favorite story about Milt was, that day the pen was to be introduced in New York, he had promised many retailers the exclusive on the ballpoint if they gave him a full-page ad in the *Times*. Boy, was Fred Gimbel surprised when he saw thirteen full-page ads that morning!"

Tom Reynolds, grandson of Edna and
Milton, son of Zelta and James Reynolds

MR. Ballpoint

Also by Gerald Everett Jones

FICTION

My Inflatable Friend: The Confessions of Rollo Hemphill

Rubber Babes: Further Misadventures of Rollo Hemphill

Farnsworth's Revenge: A Rollo Hemphill Misadventure

Boychik Lit

Christmas Karma

Bonfire of the Vanderbilts

NONFICTION

How to Lie with Charts

The Death of Hypatia and the End of Fate

MR. Ballpoint

Gerald Everett Jones

LaPuerta

Santa Monica, California

LaPuerta Books and Media

Email: info@lapuerta.tv

The characters and events of this story are inspired by a true story, based mainly on publicly available sources, but this novel is a work of fiction. Certain characters and events, as well as most of the dialogue, have been invented by the author for dramatic purposes. As well, certain actual persons have been consolidated in fictional characters, also for dramatic purposes. All references to actual public figures, such as celebrities and politicians, as well as corporations and brand-name products, are presented as parody and satire, with humorous intent.

TRADEMARKS: The author has attempted throughout this book to distinguish proprietary trademarks from descriptive terms by following the capitalization style used by the trademark owner. Any product trademarks, service marks, and registered trademarks appearing herein are the properties of their respective owners and are hereby acknowledged.

Lyrics to the original swing version of the Jack Owens song "I Got a Rocket in My Pocket," also known as "The Rocket Song," are © 1946 by Reynolds Pen Co. and used by permission. The "rock 'n roll version" in the text is original by the author.

LaPuerta trade paperback edition ISBN: 978-0-9965438-2-8
Kindle edition: 978-0-9856227-5-6

Library of Congress Control Number: 2014904753

Cover and interior design by Gary Palmatier, Ideas to Images

LaPuerta is an imprint of La Puerta Productions www.lapuerta.tv

In fond memory of
Zelta and James Reynolds

S ometimes you wonder how a thing started. The ball-point pen, for example. Everybody has one. Nowadays they're so cheap they're throwaways, like disposable razors. But time was, they were a luxury item, an expensive gift for that white-collar executive in your life who was on a rocket-ship ride to the top.

My name is Jim Reynolds and, seriously, I was trained as an engineer. I should have stuck to that. I really should have. All joking aside.

So there I was in May of 1947, standing just outside the Oval Office. Yep, the one that's inside the White House. Where else is there an oval office? There's a novel idea. I really wonder if there's another one somewhere. I mean, the President doesn't exactly have a patent on the idea, right?

It was amazing to be there for a lot of reasons. Mainly, I thought it was impossible because the President must be an incredibly busy guy, and even though the war had been officially over for a while, helping Europe rebuild and keeping a careful eye on the Russians no doubt took up a lot of his time. Even after we had the appointment set with him, I wondered whether we'd be able to meet at all when I read in the paper that the White House was undergoing renovations. They'd moved the Trumans over to Blair House across the street, and I worried that if we were so lucky as to get in front of him, it might be in a hallway somewhere for about a minute. But it turned out that the Oval Office itself was still open for business every day. While work on the residence was going on, Mr. Truman and Bess slept over at Blair House, and the Secret Service took him back and forth each day to his office.

Anyhow, I was standing there because I was too nervous to sit. And I was there, not because of anything I did, not really, but because of what my father did. Or didn't do. Or didn't necessarily *mean* to do.

It'll take a while to explain.

So seated behind the desk in front of me was Winifred, President Truman's personal secretary. She wasn't much of a looker, but then you wouldn't expect her to be. She was friendly enough, extremely well done up I should say, but she came across as efficient and no-nonsense. You'd know he'd have insisted on that, if you knew him, which I didn't. I didn't even vote for him later in '48, but that's another story, too.

Winifred was one of those iron-fist-in-a-velvet-glove types. Sweet, sincere smile, but she could cut you like a razor. Truman was running behind on his appointments that day, not a situation I thought she'd have approved of, but I'm sure she managed it well enough, with him being about as stubborn as a Missouri mule, or so they said. Didn't make me any more calm about meeting him, that's for sure.

"How much longer, do you think?" I asked her.

"Oh, just a few minutes," she said. "He's just signing a bill."

A lump came into my throat. I was nervous enough already, but the next thought I had terrified me in all kinds of new ways.

There must be a lot of dignitaries in there, including members of Congress. Reporters, too, for sure. *Way to fail*—in front of a crowd! Would he invite any of them to hang around after he asked for us to be shown in? Was there maybe another exit so they wouldn't all stampede through here? If not and they poured out, should I be standing or sitting? Sitting, it seemed to me, would be a good plan, and don't stick your legs out.

"He wouldn't, ah, use a ballpoint to sign anything important, would he?"

She gave me the oddest look. And just then, I realized I hadn't urinated for about four hours.

"Ah, you got a restroom?" I asked.

She gave me one of those silent, angled-wrist directions which indicated the general route to the toilet. I assumed the Secret Service would be following me, but I didn't mind. You have to do what you have to do. I bet lots of people have that problem right before they march into the Oval Office.

So I was at the urinal, about to let fly, and of course that's when you relax whether you want to or not. My mind popped right out of the moment, and I remembered that other time, the much more momentous time, at least from my personal viewpoint, when I was doing the same thing, right before that other big thing in my life came in on a whirlwind.

ᕦᕤ

So it was late May of 1944, and I was at the urinal in the student union at Stanford. Not a worry in the world, mind you. I had all my credits. I was going to graduate. I was a little concerned about what came next but not overly so. It wasn't a bad feeling at all.

I just started to let fly and this guy Dirk Davis glided into the stall next to me. Now, I didn't know him. Not really. I did know him by reputation. He was on the football team, which I definitely was not, not really. I was a cheerleader, and that, too, is another story. But I certainly knew *of* him, and although he wasn't strictly first string, he was a force. A force to be reckoned with. That much, I knew.

He had those chiseled good looks. You know the kind. He could probably whistle and have anything, was my thought.

So as he—oh so nonchalantly—started pissing a rope, he began to chat me up.

"Hey," he said.

"Hey," I said back, pretending it was no big deal talking to him in this casual way, even though my stream was barely a trickle at that point. I wasn't the only male cheerleader. It was kind of a tradition. But you never knew what some other guy was going to think about that. Especially a guy on the team who maybe thought of cheerleaders in short skirts as some kind of snack you have before the big game.

Was that a chuckle? Can it be you don't think much of male cheerleaders? Well, let me tell you, and here I am getting seriously ahead of my story, I got a U.S. president elected because of my cheerleading ability. Bear with me here. It was 1952, after a lot of this story takes place (but not before it ends), and I was on the dais at the Republican National Convention at the International Amphitheater in Chicago. It was a foregone conclusion that they would nominate Gen. Dwight D. Eisenhower, the war hero, for their presidential candidate. But the convention was dead-locked on the decision about who his running mate would be. To make matters more interesting, this was to be the last "brokered" convention—where even the big deals get negotiated in backrooms. That's because it was the first convention to be televised, and after that, the public had to see for themselves how roll-call votes by state determined the outcome. So there I was, an enthusiastic supporter of Ike's, and here was this big crowd on the floor in front of me with nothing to do because some cigar-chomping pols in the back room were still arguing about the VP nomination. So one of the bigwigs, who knew of my career at Stanford, said, "Lead 'em in a cheer, Jim." So I got up, and for a solid half-hour I roused the crowd in yelling, "I like Ike!" over and over and over and over again, until the deal in the closet got done. In the end, Richard M. Nixon, the senator from California, was nominated from the floor *unanimously*. And then, of course, he went on not only to serve as VP but also as president, after losing to JFK and then staging an amazing comeback, only to end up resigning as a result of the Watergate scandal. Now, think what you want about whether I should have stayed in bed that day in 1952, but I have a letter on White House stationery from Nixon when he was sitting there in the Oval Office where Truman is at the beginning of my story here, thanking me for making it possible for him to be elected to the highest office in the land.

Don't believe me? Watch the movie *MacArthur* with Gregory Peck. In it there's a news clip from the convention. Watch very carefully because it's only a second or two, and you'll see me leading that cheer.

But I digress. Back at the old urinal, I obviously didn't know my own strength. In fact, I was pretty intimidated by this second-string fullback. But it gets better (actually worse, then better).

"Damn," Dirk said, "it feels good."

I was thinking he's an animal, chatting about his bodily functions, but I wasn't going to say it.

"You said it," I said.

He laughed. "Graduation, I mean."

"Oh," I said, glad that he wasn't rhapsodizing on the joys of taking a leak.

"Know what I'm going to do?" he grinned, looking over at me as if he'd won some kind of sweepstakes.

"Engineering?" I replied, thinking it was as good a guess as any.

"You bet," he said. "I'm going to get a job at Hughes Aircraft and propose to Zelta Burrows."

Panic! Red alert! Battle stations!

I'd voided about half my bladder, but there was no time to lose. I stanched the flow, zipped up, shot him a manful grin, and got out of that restroom in a hurry.

I found Zelta in the dining hall bussing tables. She didn't look particularly surprised to see me.

Hoo boy, she was beautiful.

"Zelta," I said, breathless. "I know we said we'd take our time and not necessarily get serious right away, but will you marry me? I need an answer *immediately.*"

I have to say I did do a good job of selling her. Too good, actually. After that, she was worried I'd turn out to be just like him—my dad, the silver-tongued devil.

☙

Let's just say he didn't make it easy for her.

The day we got married was eventful and memorable, and the things I particularly remember I wish hadn't happened. Such is life.

We decided, or she planned and I agreed, to hold the ceremony in the backyard of her parents' home in Pasadena.

What with the war and the general austerity, people didn't spend a lot on those kinds of things back then. Her father was a doctor, and they had a pretty nice place, and the back lawn was about as lush as those English gardens you see in magazines, so a person could do a whole lot worse.

I was standing with the minister and a gawky maid of honor I hadn't met, underneath a flowered trellis. The thing was supposed to have started some time ago, but as they say in the theater, we were holding curtain for late arrivals.

Meaning my mother and father, who were supposedly on their way in a taxi from the airport.

They were winding up one of his business trips to South America, stopping in Cuba on the way back. There was a time he used his own plane for these jaunts, but thankfully for the sake of my mother's willingness to accompany him, he'd sold it years ago. Even now that he had to fly commercial, he still wanted his own plane. Fool that I was, I thought it would never happen.

I didn't call him Dad, by the way. I called him Milt, as everyone else did. Milton Reynolds was a legend in his own time, even before he was a legend for the pen and all the rest. He just got out of bed that way, believed it, and the world never contradicted him.

I found out later that he was giving the cab driver directions, and all the wrong ones. He'd been in Los Angeles on sales trips about a thousand times. After all, Gottschalks had stores here.

From my vantage point under the trellis, I could see Zelta primping on the back porch of the house, ready to take her father's arm and be led down the grassy aisle. Dr. Monty Burrows was a heart surgeon, a decisive man, and he was not accustomed to any manner of hesitation. When it was time to cut, dammit, he cut. She told me later how it went.

"Zelta," he said. "This man Reynolds is a..."

"A what?" she shot back.

"A...*salesman*," he spat out. "They say he's made an ungodly amount of money. In *wartime*."

There were people supposedly making fortunes selling watered-down penicillin on the black market. A doctor would not approve of that, of course. But Milton was not in that category at all. I mean, maybe he was a bit agnostic about the rules, but he wasn't breaking any laws. At least, I didn't think he was. Not back then.

"I don't care what his father does," she huffed. "*Jim* is an engineer."

It was about then she peeked around the bushes and beamed reassuringly at me. We exchanged a pantomime kiss as Monty smirked. I gave her the old spiral-wrist thing as an indication to hurry up. No use waiting for Milt, was my opinion.

Taking her cue from me, she told him, "We can't wait forever. Let's go."

Monty gave the high-sign to his wife Flora, who cranked up the old Victrola and dropped the needle on a scratchy wedding march. It was beautiful, and I actually choked back a tear or two.

"Son of a salesman is a salesman," Monty quipped to her *sotto voce* as he led her toward me. "Mark my words."

She should have. She really should have.

∽

We were duly hitched. It took about ten minutes. And we didn't spend much time chatting with the folks in the house.

About a dozen or so guests threw rice as we ran out toward a decorated Chevy coupe at the curb. We'd planned to spend the night at a little rented cabin in the mountains above Malibu. I mean to tell you, I couldn't wait. In my natural anticipation about what came next, I naturally forgot about Milt. It wasn't that I didn't care, but I knew we'd catch up with him sooner or later, and he'd have the last word, as usual. Something clever to say, all charm, as if missing my wedding was no more than a blip in the flow of time. Which, if you took the long view, it was, more or less.

But right then a cab pulled up with a screech.

Milt jumped out, ran straight up to Monty, and thrust out his hand.

"Dr. Burrows, sir," he said, and I had no idea how he knew which guy because they hadn't met until now. Then he turned beaming to Flora, getting it right again, and starts in, "And you must be—"

"— Late," Monty snapped.

There was a long moment of painful silence. Too long. My mother, Edna, appeared at Milt's side. The cabbie was right behind her, pushing a cart loaded down with luggage and a case of liquor.

Spying the case, Milt said, "Let's all have a drink!"

Monty saw it, too, something only a bar owner would recognize in wartime, and asked, "What have you got there?"

That was Milt's cue. Ice officially broken. He threw an arm around Monty's shoulders and led him back into his own house like he was the host.

Zelta and I had retraced our steps, joining the crowd as they headed back in.

"The finest Jamaican rum, my good man," Milt said. "Little wedding present from Juan Batista. What a guy. Did you know we're just in from Havana?"

I had Zelta by one arm and Monty took the other.

He asked her like a poker player throwing down his winning hand, "Happy now?"

As Milt must have figured, it didn't take that group long to guzzle up enough of his expensive rum to get a party going. I don't know how many of them had planned to stay, but they all did, sure enough.

After everyone was nicely lit up, I don't know whose idea it was to start a game of charades. I do remember Milt's performance. Vividly.

He pantomimed a movie reel, thumbed a hitch-hike, then fanned his butt with his hand.

They were all stumped.

All but Zelta. "Gone with the Wind," she sighed.

"That's my gal," Milt said, jabbing his fist at her. "Smart as a whip," he said, turning to Monty. "You didn't waste your money on Stanford."

Monty beamed back, and this time it was genuine. He knew he had fathered the school's prize catch.

I'd had plenty to drink, but I wasn't caught up in the fun. I was wondering when that moment would come when I wished to be anywhere else but here. Milt strolled over and took my arm, drawing me aside.

"Jim, boy," he cooed. "Cheer up. You're getting lucky tonight."

He was right about that, I still had reason to hope. But then, I didn't want to give him the satisfaction.

"What's the matter?" he asked. "The plane was late, the cabbie got lost, but you got a gorgeous gal and everybody's fine!"

It took me a while, but eventually I got out, "They all think you're…some kind of…I don't know…*huckster.*"

"I am!" he bellowed. "And proud of it." Then he added, "And you'll be better than me."

I knew he was trying to cheer me up, but this was the wrong speech and Zelta's worst fear.

"You're angry," he went on, dropping his voice again. "That's understandable. Ah, I know what!"

He turned his back for the briefest moment, then opened his coat and thrust out his ample stomach. Zelta glided over to watch. She wasn't used to his antics, but you could tell she suspected it was another of his gags.

"Go ahead," he challenged me, raising his voice so the others heard. "Take your best shot."

The room went quiet.

She was close enough I could say to her out of their earshot, "We used to do this a lot. He loves it."

"You'll feel better," Milton said. "I promise."

Even though I knew he had an iron gut, and even though I always pulled my punches when we clowned around like this, I hesitated. Something in the glint in his eye made me wonder how this time would be different. He was like that, sly but telltale. He had more fun when you were at least partly in on the joke.

Zelta shot me a look. "If you don't, I will."

You know, there are regrets in life, things you wish you could take back. This one took the prize.

I hauled off and slammed my fist into his stomach. Not all that hard, mind you. But hard enough, maybe harder than I intended to.

There was, as you'd expect, a collective gasp, and all eyes were on Milt.

Unfazed, he smiled broadly. Too broadly.

And then, at the corner of his mouth, there was a trickle of blood.

And then a gush, all over his white dress shirt.

Everyone was horrified as he stumbled back, fell onto the couch, and slumped over, as if he'd expired.

Zelta looked over at me in panic. Terrified, I looked over at my Mom.

Mildly annoyed, Mom looked down at Milt. "That's enough, dear," she soothed.

After a dramatic beat, he came back to life. He sat up and spit out a sticky-red cellophane packet, which he waved in my direction.

"Gotcha, young man!" he wheezed. "A new vegetable-based printer's ink. Ran into the inventor over a friendly Scotch and got the world distribution rights."

To everyone's amazement, he got up, walked back over to me, and gave me an affectionate slap on the back.

"I tried catsup," he explained, "but it wasn't realistic."

Zelta looked over at Monty, whose own worst suspicions were nowhere near bad enough.

2

We had our blissful night in Malibu, but of course it wasn't all that much of a honeymoon. I thought Milt might have staked us for an exotic trip, but instead they invited us to visit them in Chicago. It was hardly a resort vacation, but we figured it would be nice enough as long as we didn't stay too long.

Another incorrect assumption.

We'd graduated in June of 1944 and been married soon after, but we didn't take Milt up on his offer right away. I had this idea I'd grab an aerospace job in California, and then Zelta wanted us to spend the holidays with her family out West. My job search wasn't successful (perhaps my expectations were too high), and even though Milt probably would have paid our way, we didn't want to be traveling back and forth across the country. So, between one thing and another, we didn't make it to Chicago until the spring of 1945.

And, like I said, we didn't plan to stay. Or, that's what we told each other. In truth, we'd stayed away because she didn't want to see him and I didn't want to face him. Our going back was a tacit admission that maybe we were running out of options.

Milt and Edna had an apartment on South Lake Shore Drive, on the edge of Hyde Park. It looked out over the water, and it was, in pretty much all respects, the high life.

As we rode up in the elevator with our one suitcase, I wanted to tell her what it was like growing up there. Just me and our housekeeper Henrietta, when they were off on their round-the-world trips. He liked to fly, which so few civilians could afford to do back then, and of course there was always a business reason. He supposedly had a lot of friends in a lot of places. But he wasn't exactly a captain of industry, at least, not outside of his own mind. Summers, they'd send me to Scout camp. I earned every merit badge there was. Twice.

She didn't understand why I didn't call him Dad, and I really couldn't explain. He was Milton Reynolds the legend, smooth-talking Milt who'd already made and lost several fortunes, most recently on the loss side but absolutely sure he would find the next big thing any day.

We stood outside their apartment door. I smoothed down my cowlick and she checked her lipstick.

She gave me one of her sterner looks. "We are staying for a few days only," she informed me. "If he asks you to work for him, say you've got an offer from Standard Oil."

"I need a job," I said, as if she didn't know. "We can't live on love." And I tried to smile.

The door opened, and there stood Milt, grinning his face off.

"You two look great," he said. Then, for my benefit, he exuded, "If New York is a glass slipper, Chicago is a work boot. Yessir, a man can make a deal in this town."

He knew why I'd come.

I was about to say something in reply, but he fawned over Zelta as he ushered us in.

"And Zel-ta! I'd almost forgotten how ravishing you are." He winked at me, actually winked. "You're a lucky boy, Jim."

"Man," Zelta shot back. "He's a lucky man. And whatever it is you're selling, we're not buying."

Hoo boy!

Milt was speechless for once, and we walked past him into the apartment.

Henrietta was holding the door, and we exchanged smiles. There's no mother like your mother, but Henrietta knew how to bake cookies. Before I could say anything, she'd taken the bag from my hand and stepped back as Mom rushed at us with outstretched arms. She was wearing one of those prim cotton frocks of hers, a new one that had probably come from the most exclusive boutique on Michigan Avenue. "Our son the engineer and his brilliant, beautiful wife!" she exclaimed as she kissed Zelta on the cheek and hugged me.

Milt was out ahead of us, gesturing expansively. Indicating the suitcase, he announced, "Henrietta will take that to the guest room. *Your* room." She was turning away when Zelta grabbed the handle and wouldn't let go.

"We're not staying," she said, and I somehow I thought we would be headed right back out. She realized she didn't mean it quite that way and said, "Not long, I mean," but she kept hold of the handle.

Then it was Milt who reached for the case. Bewildered, Henrietta let go, and he and Zelta had it between them. "Nonsense," Milt said as he stared her down while he flashed his big grin. "You'll stay until you find your own place." Then, turning his expectant gaze to me, he announced, "Tomorrow, Jim and I are paying a call on the Goldblatt brothers."

Zelta's tightened her grip and looked over at me, as if waiting for my speech of defiance, which, of course, never came.

"What are we selling?" I ventured to ask.

"These guys run a multimillion-dollar operation," he said, almost but not quite forgetting to hold his own in the tug of war. "We'll have lunch in their private dining room, cigars, a spirited negotiation among gentlemen…"

Zelta could tell from my expression I wasn't about to contradict him. She let go of the case, and Milt passed it back to Henrietta, who dutifully left to carry it into the guest room.

છ

Henrietta served us a light dinner and there was no more talk of life goals or plans. Just polite chit-chat interspersed with awkward silences. We excused ourselves early and went to bed.

As Zelta and I got ready to turn in, I heard my parents' muffled voices on the other side of the wall. I heard Mom call out, "Milton!" And then she said "Please stop" and I thought she said "facing" but it must have been "pacing."

I grabbed a water glass from the nightstand and pressed it to the wall, as I'd seen William Powell do in one of those Thin Man movies. Zelta shot me a disapproving frown, but it worked, and I could hear the rest of the conversation pretty clearly.

Milt huffed, "Do you remember that time we visited him at summer camp? He sulks in with a bloody nose? He never learned how to stick up for himself."

Had he expected me to disagree with him? In front of everyone else? And surely he hadn't wanted me to punch him in the nose. Not after my last performance.

Mom said, "Dear, Zelta seems like a sensible girl. She's not going to hit him. Even if he deserves it."

"The boy needs his sleep," Milt grumbled. "I'm making a man out of him tomorrow."

Well, that was that. We didn't dare make the slightest noise. Zelta got to sleep quicker than I did.

The next morning, when I was all lathered up shaving, Milt came up behind me and addressed me in the mirror.

"Six a-m and you feel like crap, right?" he chuckled.

As I studied the shadows under my eyes, I could only agree, "Uh-huh."

"That's the secret of successful selling."

"You don't say" was all I managed to grunt as I resumed my razor strokes.

"I hate to get up in the morning," Milt admitted, as if it was news, and I knew he didn't think that. "I look worse than you. I see my sad, sorry, puffy face in that mirror. I think how warm and cozy it was back in bed, and I say to myself, 'Somebody's going to *pay* for this!'"

After breakfast, I put on the tie and sport coat I was glad I'd remembered to bring. I didn't even own a suit. Milton was standing expectantly in the living room, dressed to the nines in a three-piece gray flannel. The tie was Italian silk. He beckoned me over to the full-length mirror in the hallway, straightened my lapels, and even took a brush to them. Then he turned me to face the mirror.

"It's all in the hands," he said as he stood behind me and shot his French cuffs. He gestured elaborately as he went on, "The expression, the *warmth*, is in the hands."

"You never told me. What are we selling?" I understandably wanted to know.

With a magician's sleight of hand, he fetched a lighter from his vest pocket and flicked on the flame.

"I got two truckloads of video lighters."

Zelta came over in time to hear me say, "Jeez, the same old crapola."

She was still in her bathrobe, but he'd captured her attention by summoning fire out of thin air.

"How is it video?" she asked.

I took the lighter from Milt and showed it to her. Its body was made of clear plastic so you could see the fluid sloshing around inside.

Quoting his familiar sales pitch, I explained, "This amazing, atomic-age lighter with the see-through fuel tank never runs out of fuel."

"That's impossible," she said, not taking her eyes off it, and, I could tell, half wondering whether Milt really could pull miracles out of his pocket.

I flipped the cap shut and handed the lighter to her. "Read the fine print," I said.

She found the inscription on the bottom in type so small she had to really squint to read it. "Never runs out of fuel… without…giving several days' notice!"

"Kind of grabs you, doesn't it?" Milt asked her, taking it back. "That one came to me—just came to me." Turning to me, he emphasized, "That's how you sell. Go after the Big Idea."

I primped and checked my lapels one more time. "Make 'em pay," I sighed. "Big Idea. Ready."

wondered why we didn't take a cab, but Milt was funny that way. He'd splurge without a thought on anything that showed or that he particularly enjoyed, but when he was behind the scenes, he scrimped, often unnecessarily, I thought. That morning, we took the State Street trolley up to the Goldblatt's store in the downtown shopping district. He lugged a big black sample case full of video lighters. He explained he'd be asking for an order for many more than that, but he wanted them to have enough of an inventory so they could put them on special that day. Never mind that they'd see it as a Christmas gift item, and I wasn't sure why we were pitching them now, in late April.

Me, I was sure they'd see us coming. I knew this wasn't his first time hawking that product. We were going to pee into the wind.

As we jumped off near the store, he set the case down on the sidewalk to catch his breath. I'd have carried it gladly, but he didn't ask me and I didn't offer. I had no idea what that much product was worth. Maybe it was a lot, and he was afraid I'd leave it somewhere.

In this spring season, the retail world was set to sell summer goods. The store window behind him was decorated around a picnic theme. The mannequins wore sunhats with big straw purses. Milt jerked a thumb in their direction, as if the little diorama explained everything.

"They'll be buying for Christmas soon," he panted. "Our timing is perfect." Off my skeptical look, he turned his attention to a sailor who was waiting at the crosswalk for the light to change. The guy was just lighting up. "What does every GI learn to do?" Milt asked me. "Smoke," he answered his own question, as if I couldn't guess, "every chance he gets. And with the shortages, there's no luxury items—precious few novelties, even."

He was right about that. Even though it looked as if the war in Europe was about over, the conflict in the Pacific was still raging and threatened to cast a pall on another holiday shopping season.

As if practicing his presentation, Milt pulled the sample lighter from his vest pocket and flicked it on in a single, deft sweep of the hand. Fascinated by the flame, he pronounced, "Every girl's gift solution. We'll kick the zip out of Zippo!"

I almost believed him, but I had to ask, "Do these things even work? I mean, for long?"

Abruptly, he flipped the lighter closed and tossed it in the air. I caught it chest-high, and for the briefest moment I felt we were a synchronized team.

"Premium merchandise," he said as he picked up his sample case and started to walk off. *"Hecho en Meh-hee-co!"*

"Hoo boy," I mumbled, as I hustled to catch up.

∾

The Goldblatt brothers, Joel and Louis, did indeed take our meeting in their executive conference room. And they did serve us—hot dogs and sodas sent up from the store lunch counter.

They seemed underwhelmed to see Milt, but they gave him an audience.

Milt had gifted each of them with cigars. Milt tried to use his sales sample to light one for Louis, but, as if worn out from our practice tries, the lighter failed three times before the flame finally caught.

I was trying to look alert and intelligent, and I didn't dare say a word. Joel was doodling on a writing pad with a shiny black pen.

After Louis took a few satisfying puffs, Milt beamed, "Nothing like a Havana."

Louis forced a smile. "You always had class, Reynolds. I give you that." Then, indicating the mustard-smeared waxed-paper leavings from our sumptuous buffet, he added, "Sorry about the stuff from the counter. Palmer House next time, on us." I thought I saw him cast a sly glance at Joel. Maybe there wouldn't be a next time?

Right then, Milt boldly asked for the order. "So, what'll it be? Say, twenty thousand units?"

Louis had a blank look, didn't answer. Milt looked over to Joel, who looked up from his drawing to take his cue from Louis, who shook his head ever so slightly.

Joel asked, "What are you talking about?"

Milt replied, "Well, I sure haven't got that many Havanas!"

No one thought it was funny. Milt was dying.

"Come on, boys," he cajoled. "How many of these little stocking stuffers are you going to move this year?"

Louis took a puff, blew it out, and asked, "This dreck's all you got?"

Staying doggedly positive, Milt said calmly to Louis, "Nobody's got novelty merchandise like this. This is premium stuff."

Joel interjected, "We took ten thousand of them last year. How many you want to buy back?"

And Louis chimed in, "If they're so great, go unload them on Marshall Field."

The two shared a laugh over that one. It was said that the high-toned Marshall Field refused to buy from Jewish vendors, and he was obviously not one of their favorite people. In retailing, there were circles within circles, and Milt, whose family name was Reinsberg, was inside theirs and couldn't get a meeting at Field's, but that's another story.

"You guys have always been top of my list," Milt said.

Joel waited for Louis, who eventually said, "What we need is something new."

"Really new," Joel added pointlessly.

"An idea that has appeal," Louis went on.

"Popular," Joel added, as if the definition needed elaboration.

"Something everybody needs," Louis continued, making it clear whatever it was would be a necessity, not a luxury.

"Can't do without," Joel added, to crystallize the point.

Milt was lost, studied his lighter, then observed, "Everybody smokes. And video, television, what's newer than that?"

Louis got out of his chair, and I thought the meeting was suddenly over. But instead, he walked over to Joel and snatched the pen out of his hand.

"This," he said emphatically. "This is what."

Milt must have thought he meant whatever was on Joel's paper. "Cartoons?" Then, Louis thrust the pen at him, and he took it, rolled it in his hand. "A fountain pen?"

"Look at it. Closely," Louis demanded.

"That's no fountain pen," Joel said importantly, and I got that interpreting his brother's opinions was something he did routinely. I also realized they must have planned to let Milt make his pitch, whatever it was, but planned to ignore it and get down to this, because there was something about this pen that had them all aflutter.

Milt was inspecting the pen and stroked the tip with his thumb. He looked puzzled, as though he'd never seen a fountain pen before. I couldn't see from where I was sitting what was so special about it.

"Joel," Louis smirked, "I don't think he gets the point, heh, heh. Find us twenty thousand of those, Reynolds."

"I give up," Milt said simply.

Louis got serious, and he was no longer teasing. "Crazy Hungarian. Biro, I think his name is," he confided quietly, as though it was a wartime secret, "comes up with this marker for printer's galleys. Can't get arrested with it until the RAF finds out the damn thing writes at high altitude."

Well, what do you know, it *was* kind of a wartime secret.

"War's going to be over, boys," Milt said.

Joel came back, "He still doesn't get it, Lou." Then he leaned over and, imparting the most closely guarded secret of all, he confided, "It's like your video *schmageggy*. Never runs out of ink."

"Not for days, not for weeks, even," Louis said, no-joke, this time echoing Joel.

Milt handed the pen to me, and I suddenly I had the flash that, as the recent engineering graduate from the prestigious halls of Stanford, perhaps I could finally find something worthwhile to say. So I proceeded to study the thing as they resumed their discussion in earnest.

"And you think people will want these?" Milt asked, as if it wasn't such a big deal.

"It's class," Louis asserted. "White-collar stuff. Personal luxury that's a necessity. And it's new. Sell for, who knows, ten bucks?"

There wasn't anything particularly complicated about the device, that I could see. But it did have a new kind of tip. It came to a rounded point. As I glided it over the tip of my finger, it left a neat line of gooey ink, not at all like the thin liquid from a fountain pen. From the feel of it, I guessed the tip was a rolling ball. That was new, all right. But I couldn't think right then how it would make such a big difference. I mean, for one thing, you couldn't dip it in an inkwell. There must be some way of taking it apart and filling it from the top. That comment about high altitude could be something.

"Ten dollars? It couldn't cost more than two bits to make," I commented, hoping I sounded like an expert. A bar of aluminum turned on a lathe, I thought. A tube. A tube with that odd-ball tip. Maybe something in the ink was special, but dyes and gelatins didn't cost much. For certain chemicals during the war, there was actually a surplus.

I could tell from Milt's wide stare that he was thinking about the profit margin, and he liked it.

"Okay, who makes them?" he demanded.

"Sixty-four-dollar question," Joel said huffily.

"Yeah," Louis said. "You find out, you tell us. We hear the guy's on the lam in Argentina."

Meaning, the Hungarian inventor guy. I borrowed Joel's pad, tore off a sheet, and used the new pen to write BIRO –

ARGENTINA? I underlined it twice. The roller pen wrote nice, real nice. Like I said, it glided. I could see how if it actually gave people pleasure to write with it, that would be a big deal in itself, whatever other practical advantages it might have.

"Newspaper guys aren't too popular in the old country these days," Joel said. In tossing off a crack about the man's emigration to Argentina, Joel had reminded us ever so subtly that the Nazis had killed off intellectuals as well as Jews. At least the war in Europe was almost over, but no one was ready to take a deep sigh of relief. They were ready to murder anyone but their own over there in the Land of the Rising Sun.

"So how'd you get it?" Milt asked.

Joel answered, "One of the buyers got it from a flyboy. Uncle Sam wants somebody to make them stateside."

Joel's offhand remarks had a way up creeping up on you. It seemed he was implying he had some information that the War Department was anticipating a long, drawn-out conflict.

It occurred to me, in that moment, that neither of them had intended in this meeting to mock Milton Reynolds. Oh, they'd teased him about the lighter all right, but it was an old joke among older friends. What I realized then, and I hadn't appreciated before, was that these serious businessmen did indeed think Milt could work miracles. They wanted this product, and evidently they wanted it badly. But they had no idea where to find it, and they were challenging Milt to either buy it or find out how to make it for them.

And yet they didn't want to sound desperate or needy, on the chance he could actually find it, and would demand too high a price.

Milt must have read the room the same way, because he told them, "Gentlemen, if Milton Reynolds can't get it, it can't be had." He waved the pen. "Mind if I keep this one?"

He started to pocket it, and Louis quickly grabbed it back.

"Get your own goddamn ballpoint pen," he said.

Well, from Lou Goldblatt's lips to God's ears.

4

Outside the Goldblatt building, an odd kind of coincidence happened. Just as Milt and I stepped out to the curb, a biplane flew overhead towing a banner, "SHOP AT MARSHALL FIELD'S." Spooky, like the guy was watching us.

At least, that's what I was thinking. But evidently it was coincidental to Milt for another reason.

"Flying Down to Rio," he sighed, his eyes tracking the plane.

"Huh?"

"It was a movie," he said. I knew, too. Starring Fred Astaire and Ginger Rogers, the dance duo that floated on clouds and never missed a step. "Your mother loved the dancing," he went on. "I loved the plane."

35

I also knew, as he knew I knew but didn't mention, that he had his own single-engine airplane years ago when I was still in short-shorts. He wasn't a pilot any more than a guy who hails a cab is a cabbie. But he loved to tool around the country in it. He called it *The Flying Printasign,* after one of the companies he started. Printasign sold printing equipment to retailers for making signs and price tags. It was still a going concern, and it was the main reason he could get face-to-face meetings with executives like the Goldblatts instead of some overworked buyer.

Speaking of Printasign, did you ever see a price tag with a sales message on it besides the product size and price? Maybe with its features and benefits as well? In retailing that's known as a "talking sign," and it was Milt's own invention, an innovation that predated the ballpoint pen by more than a decade. The purpose of the talking price tag (which he sometimes called the "silent salesperson") was to induce shoppers to buy *one more item* before they left the store. To this day, that's the main purpose of all in-store sales messages.

Milt was fond of saying, "Printasign was the bread and butter that kept the home fires burning." He had a talent for mixing metaphor, which he did fearlessly. In those early days as I went along on selling trips, this particular trait of his made him seem uneducated and sometimes downright rude. It was years later when customers would remember and repeat such sayings to me that I would realize nothing sears the brain quite so effectively as the illogical juxtaposition of two unrelated concepts.

He wouldn't ever explain it this way, mind you. He just *did* it.

The video lighter thing was a kind of sideline. He wasn't into peddling those so much as he was always buying up odd-lot novelties of any kind in the hope he could turn a quick profit. He'd said as much to Lou and Joel during the meeting. Retailing in wartime was all about dealing with shortages, and luxury gift items were especially hard to find.

The plane was a great, memorable promotion angle, and it was a total business write-off. Legend had it in the company that Milt's favorite sales ploy was to take some retailer up in it, pitch the deal, then not too subtly refuse to land until the guy agreed to sign. (Knowing him, he'd make a joke out of it. A joke the other guy would hardly find funny.) But maybe it was only a story, a story he loved telling on himself.

He fished in his pocket and pulled out a wad of bills. He pulled off a couple, and instead of handing me some spending money, he gave me what was left of the wad. A lot of dough, from the look of it.

"Here," he said. "Get a cab to the airport and hustle me a ticket to Buenos Aires."

I was bewildered, to say the least. "Uh, which flight?"

"There's a war on, in case you haven't noticed. Any flight."

I was afraid it was a tall order, too tall. But tall orders were all he gave.

"What if there aren't any seats?" I asked.

"There probably won't be any," he huffed. "Do I have to spell it out for you?"

Yeah, he did. None of my engineering courses or in fact anything I'd studied in school could have remotely prepared me to be Milt's errand boy, let alone his son.

"Find somebody with a ticket and talk them out of it," he said, as if people did it every day.

Then he pulled the pen—Joel Goldblatt's Myles Aircraft pen—from his breast pocket.

"I got a feeling this is the Big Idea," he beamed.

"You swiped his pen," I said, but not so loudly that anyone else on the street could hear.

It was not exactly a mixed metaphor, but something along those same lines, when Milt later bragged we "stole the ballpoint pen fair and square."

☙

Milt was on a plane to Rio, then on to Buenos Aires, after I'd successfully negotiated a ticket for him by the unheard-of method of walking up to the Pan Am ticket counter and asking for it. Right now I figured he'd be somewhere over Central America. My mother had taken her cue and headed up to Evanston to play cards at her women's club, and she'd given Henrietta the day off.

So Zelta and I had the apartment all to ourselves. I figured now was the perfect time to get right down to it, and I'd expected she would be just as eager.

Except she wasn't.

When I started to go at it hot and heavy, rounding second base, as it were, she flopped over on her back and let out a big, disgusted puff of air.

"I can't believe you went with him on that sales call."

"Zel-ta," I tried not to whine. "We haven't done it since we've been here!"

"Pardon me if I stifle my screams of passion while your mother plays Mahjong in the next room."

"She's playing bridge on the North Shore. That was a good excuse for yesterday."

"I mean, for all we know they listen through the wall," she continued, as if she hadn't heard me. Never mind I was the one guilty of eavesdropping, but she had a point where

Milt was concerned. "And then," she fumed, "sending you out like some errand boy. The next thing you know, he'll be hiring you into the business."

She looked at me as though the thought was obviously ridiculous, and then when I didn't say anything right away, she realized it wasn't.

She sat up in the bed, pulling the sheets around her. "Jim Reynolds! Did he rope you into some kind of deal? Tell me you didn't sign anything."

"I didn't say yes absolutely. He thinks he's found the Big Idea." Besides, I thought, what difference would signing make? Any promise to Milt has its own ironclad guarantee.

She jumped up, grabbed her dressing gown, and pulled it on.

"I can think of some big ideas," she said as she cinched up, as if tying off her charms for the foreseeable future. "Aircraft. Railroads. You're an engineer. What happens when the war is over? If you wait, you'll have that much more competition. Those GIs have experience. They've got scars, and purple hearts, and... "

"And I've got...allergies," I admitted. She knew the story well enough why Uncle Sam didn't want me, but she'd never thrown it back at me.

"I'm sorry," she said. "I didn't mean..."

She didn't need an explanation and I didn't owe her one, but saying it as I moved to her gave me time to get my arms around the silk robe. "I could be out on recon, sneeze at the wrong time, and you'd be a widow. A gorgeous, eligible widow. I said I couldn't allow that, and the Army agreed."

Then I said, "I can't leave him now," as I pulled her to me.

She put her palm on my chest and pushed me gently away. It wasn't so much a rejection as a pause for consideration. "He's made and lost more than we'll ever have." She was stalling. "What did he start with? Used Model T tires? Then it was prefab houses? War surplus?" Then she must have remembered his performance at our wedding party. "Vegetable-based printing ink!"

The color rose in her face, and her anger made her that much sexier. I kissed her, and this time she didn't push me away.

"Darling," I said. "I have a woody, and somebody's going to pay for this."

If she had a comeback for the argument, she forgot it when I chased her under the covers and she started to giggle.

"How long will he be gone?"

She was a gazelle and I was a hungry lion. She had no chance.

"Long enough to find some guy they call 'Odd-Ball Biro' and talk him out of whatever he's got."

5

I can imagine how it went with Biro. Milt spun the story for us when he got back. Of course, I was used to his penchant for exaggeration and unfounded optimism. And later events made it apparent that he didn't necessarily come back with everything he'd expected to get.

László Jozsef Biro ran a small print shop on a side street in downtown Buenos Aires. Back in Budapest, he'd been a journalist. Just two years ago in 1943, he and his business-partner brother Gyorgy had emigrated, for several compelling reasons. First off, they were Jews. And they could afford to leave. And it wasn't just what the German occupiers wanted László *not* to write. It was also what they wanted him to *print.*

It was László Biro's affinity for printing technology that had inspired the pen's invention, which he had exhibited at the Budapest International Fair as far back as 1931. Years earlier, when he was an apprentice pressman, he'd noticed that gelatinous newsprint ink dried much quicker than fountain-pen ink, which had to be watery just to flow through the tip. He guessed that the newsprint ink would be a much better handwriting medium, but he had to develop a rolling-ball mechanism to get it to flow onto the paper. Gyorgy, a chemist, was fully a co-creator of the pen because he was the one to formulate a new ink that had just the right combination of properties. It not only flowed freely through the roller-ball tip but also dried almost as quickly as it was deposited on the paper.

The Biro brothers started a business venture to launch the pen, which they named the Birome, patented in Paris in 1939. But wartime Europe wasn't exactly the right place to market a consumer novelty, much less a personal luxury item that would have to sell for more than a week's ration of milk.

Argentina welcomed them, as it did so many of their countrymen in those days, but their pen manufacturing scheme stayed mostly a sideline. Setting up his print shop in a tolerant but strictly Catholic country, László spent most of his time designing and typesetting wedding invitations and announcements for first communions and *quinceañeras.*

Milt arrived in Buenos Aires on a bright day in early May—it was fall south of the equator—and the gas fumes from the cars crowding the city streets were borne away by gentle breezes. This place was bustling—the Chicago of South America was how he thought of it. No war to distract or distress folks and lots of foreigners arriving with money in their pockets. It would be a good place to knock back a drink or two, he was also thinking, no doubt.

Milton Reynolds let himself into the Biro Engraving and Fine Printing shop and, finding no one behind the counter, stepped into the back room. He found a balding, middle-aged man in a rumpled suit asleep at his composing machine.

"Ah, excuse me?" Milton cooed. "Mr. Biro? Lászlo Biro?"

Biro snorted and looked up, half awake. *"Nein. Biro ist nicht hier!"* His hair-triggered response was a consequence of suffering oppression, an acquired talent for self defense in simple words the oppressor would understand and, hopefully, believe.

"You're not Lászlo Biro?" Milton continued, in English, which was the only language he had at his command, but also one he was sure wouldn't be associated with head-knocking *politzei*.

Biro rubbed his eyes, put on his spectacles, and, now fully awake, took a good appraising look at his visitor.

"You are with the underground?" he asked quietly, in accented English.

Milt thrust out his hand. "Milton Reynolds from the States. Delighted to make your acquaintance!"

Biro grasped the offered hand cautiously, as if trying on the idea of a greeting, and bade Milt to sit.

"You're not from the government? The diplomats and the spies, they also speak English."

"Businessman," Reynolds proudly assured him as, by way of explanation, he pulled the pen he'd lifted off Joel Goldblatt from his suit-coat pocket. But, always the showman, Milt didn't hand it over to Biro right away. Instead, he held it in front of him, caressed it and admired it, as though it were Merlin's magic wand. In reverent tones, he pronounced, "I've come a long way to meet the inventor of this. He is a very clever, a very *fortunate* man."

Biro wasn't necessarily buying the pitch, but he apparently shared Milt's fascination for the pen. "May I see?"

Milt handed the pen to him, carefully, as though mishandling might set off fireworks or the end of the world as we know it.

Biro took it delicately, pulling it close to his glasses to squint at its fine detail. He had obviously never seen this version before. "The British model. Our partner, Henry Martin, is English. He made a deal with Myles Aircraft. They make the pens for the pilots."

He pulled an envelope from a drawer, laid it on the desk, and used the pen to write "Milton Reynolds" on it in well-formed cursive, spelling the name correctly.

"Very nice," he muttered. "Almost as good as a Birome."

Of course, Milt had known about the Myles Aircraft deal because the Goldblatts had told him. But he'd carefully parsed Biro's every word, and now he was worried. "You *sold* the rights to an aircraft company?"

"No, no." Biro actually patted Milt's arm reassuringly. "Only in England and only for the Air Force. Not many units, mind you, and not much money, very frankly."

Never very good at poker, Milt had to force himself not to smile. He didn't want to rush it, either, knowing that he'd need to balance his show of enthusiasm for the genius of the product with a cool-headed assessment of its acquisition cost. "I'm prepared to make you an offer—a generous offer—for the North American manufacturing rights."

Biro smiled gently, and he seemed not the least bit surprised. After a moment, he said, "You flatter me. But I cannot."

Milt suspected he'd run up against a skilled negotiator here. And there was something about wartime that honed the bartering skills of not only businessmen but everyone. In that moment, he decided that haggling wouldn't win this man's heart. Milt was a genuine Yankee in a tropical linen suit with a dandy straw hat he'd bought just for this trip, and there could be no doubt he was a man of style and substance, an international entrepreneur of the first order. He was the man fated to take this dream, this ambitious little prototype, and put millions of the gleaming devices into the worsted pockets of every white-collar professional on the planet. He could afford to be bold.

He must show he could do what no one else could. He decided, therefore, to present his best offer: "I'm offering cash. Ten thousand dollars. I can have it wired from my bank in Chicago. You can have it tomorrow."

Milt could see right away that Biro was no poker player. The little man looked enormously pleased. Milt was sure he'd scored, and at the right price.

But Biro's response was a non sequitur. "You came all the way from Chicago?"

Milt thought then that Biro was stalling, calculating a counter while unable to hide his delight.

"The percentage," Milt suggested, sweetening the deal. "I should have mentioned the royalty. Do you have a patent?"

Biro waved his hand dismissively. "Oh, yes. We took care of that. All the papers. My brother and I, in Paris, right before the war."

"We could be very generous on the royalty," Milt insisted. "Very. Generous." He'd hold the line on the down payment, because cash was cash, and he had to keep some in reserve for his manufacturing startup costs. But he was prepared to dicker over the percentage, as long as his costs were covered. And a crafty lawyer could word it right, so that the venture wouldn't necessarily go into profit for a good, long while. This would be a good deal. He could feel it coming.

But Biro just shook his head. "Out of the question," he said, barely audible, almost apologetically.

Milt was angry now. This guy was playing him, and doing a terrible job of it. He did, after all, come all the way from Chicago. And he knew this was a stellar offer. Bona fide international entrepreneurs don't waltz into your little print shop every day and just plunk down gold like this. After all!

"Listen," Milt said, getting up because he was antsy now, and also so he'd have room to gesture expansively. "Every businessman, every homemaker, every school kid in the great big U S of A needs one of your miracle ball-point pens! Who knows, maybe even two. Now, I'm kind of strapped for cash at the moment—but I'm going all out here. *Name your price!*"

He'd blurted it out. No taking it back. He resolved to play more poker.

"Name it," he went on, "and you'll get the ten thousand tomorrow and we'll pay the rest from profits. You can't do better than that." He might be promising the Moon, but he wouldn't have to deliver it tomorrow.

"You are a persuasive man," Biro mused, and once again Milt thought he'd scored. And he was sure he'd hit home when Biro admitted, "Your offer is indeed more than acceptable."

Milt broke into a broad grin and actually hugged the little guy. But then, he realized Biro still hadn't mentioned a number.

"So," Milt beamed, gripping Biro firmly by the shoulders, "shall we say ten percent of the net?"

Biro shook his head again. You'd think his dog had died.

I don't believe this guy! Milt was thinking.

"What is it now?" Milt demanded, his patience at an end.

"Your offer is indeed good," Biro allowed. "We should have met sooner."

"What?" was all Milt could find to say.

"And you came all the way from Chicago," Biro sighed, sounding genuinely impressed. "I have a prior commitment. Not so good a deal, even. With a company in America. Eversharp. A license. But exclusive, you see. Exclusive, sorry."

In point of fact, Biro knew more than he was telling. His partner had actually licensed the patent to Eberhard Faber, a U.S. manufacturer of pencils. But, for various reasons, Faber didn't get around to actually producing a pen. So they turned around and cut a deal with Eversharp.

In front of Milton, Biro was at a loss. Milt was exasperated that the fellow had taken such a roundabout way to impart this crucial information. But he could also see that Biro was basking in the attention. Someone of importance had traveled a very long way to acknowledge him for his history-making achievement. He wasn't about to send the man away without giving his offer a full hearing.

"Henry went there," Biro began, a storyteller now. "New York. He brought me a whistle that looks like the Statue of Liberty."

For a moment, Milton was crushed. This pen thing seemed like the Big Idea, but Eversharp had beaten him to the punch. *Damn!* It occurred to him that a well-worded telegram could have saved him the expense of the trip. So much for initiative. Ah well, if you're going to do the impossible, you have to do it right away.

Milt was not about to waste the trip. Wouldn't South America be the perfect place to peddle his novelty items? Reflexively, he reached again into his coat pocket, produced a video lighter, and handed it with a flourish to Biro. "Latest thing in the States," he said. "With my compliments."

Biro, the technologist, was enthralled. He flicked it open and studied the flame.

"This is a new invention?"

"It never runs out of fuel," Milt pronounced brazenly.

"Amazing," muttered Biro, still studying the flame. "From Chicago."

Seeing Biro's reaction to the lighter, Milton judged correctly that the man was more of an engineer than a salesman, and he saw a glimmer of hope. Perhaps this game was not over after all.

"László," Milt said, working up a comradely tone, "just what is the basis of your patent?"

And as Milt had guessed, Biro was delighted to have the opportunity to explain.

"Capillary action!" Biro said in a hush. "You know, when you drink *der spritzer* with a straw?" He turned the envelope over and, using his own Birome pen, drew a diagram as Milt watched intently. "Like so, the ink flows out through the tube, like sucking on a straw. A function of the viscosity of the ink and the cross-sectional area of the tube."

Once again, Biro had not told the whole story. The capillary action part was entirely true. He and Gyorgy had indeed secured a patent. What Milt did not appreciate at the time, and perhaps he never did, was that Biro did not have a patent on the roller-ball idea. American John Loud had come up with that invention, which he patented in 1888. The idea was never exploited, and even now in 1945, the ballpoint patent had long since expired. No one held a patent to the ballpoint concept, and never could.

All that said, in theory, no pen manufacturer would be able to copy *Biro's* design without infringing on his patent for capillary action. So his patent was as valid as his ink-flow process was valuable. And that should have been enough to stop Milt in his tracks. Of course, it didn't. Milt had enough experience to know patent suits took a long time. And all he wanted was to make a fortune by Christmas.

For some reason, it annoyed Milt the way the little guy said *tyooooob*. Ah, well. He looked respectfully at the envelope, a historic document now, took it, folded it neatly, and tucked it into his coat pocket, along with Biro's pen.

"Viscosity, eh?" Milt said, not knowing in the least what the word meant but memorizing Biro's explanation literally. "Mr. Biro, I believe I've taken up enough of your time."

For his part, Biro still could not take his eyes off the lighter. The flame was out now, and he fondled the case, turning it over and over in his hand. Impulsively, as Milt eased his way toward the door, Biro grabbed a magnifying glass from his desk and held it up, squinting as he searched for the secret mechanism of its eternal flame.

Milt was just stepping from the room as he heard Biro say, "It says this lighter was made in Mexico."

Maybe it was just coincidence, but Milt goes off on a business trip and the war in Europe ends. Later in life he'd hobnob with nabobs and potentates, and who's to say he didn't help decide the fate of the world? He'd certainly think he could manage it.

It was May 8, 1945, Victory in Europe—VE Day. There was a picture in the paper of some swabbie bending a dame over to lay a wet one on her in the midst of a jubilant crowd in Times Square. Any excuse to cop a feel. But when you thought about it, and actually it took no thought at all, nothing would ever feel quite so good. I mean, I'd already gotten laid for the first time. So the only other bigger thrill I could imagine was hearing I was a father—or St. Peter say, "Come on in," but I was prepared to wait for that one.

(Mom had converted to Christian Science and Milt was a profound I-don't-knowist, so I'd have to ask her whether she thought I had that to look forward to.) Then again, I supposed the birth of a child could figure in there somewhere, but Zelta and I hadn't experienced that yet, and I wasn't sure we were quite ready. Not that we couldn't stand the joy, but we were not eager for the responsibility—and the expense—that were sure to follow.

Zelta and I ducked into the movie house, and there was so much necking and groping, I'm not sure any of us could tell you what the feature was. Hedy Lamar or Rita Hayworth. Clark Gable or Monty Clift. Claude Rains or Sidney Greenstreet or that little weasel Peter Lorre—the guys you loved to hate. Or maybe it was Charlie Chan. We still had plenty of reason to hate the Japs, even though Charlie Chan was supposed to be Chinese but the actor who played him, Warner Oland, wasn't Asian in any way at all. (He was Swedish, in fact.)

But all eyes were on the screen for the Movietone News. Cities were still smoking from the bombings. Filthy little waifs were crying their eyes out because they couldn't find their mommies or begging for scraps, or dying in ditches. Skeletons with skin on their bones stood and by some miracle or maybe just force of will hadn't yet joined the pile of corpses behind them. Seated comfortably in darkened theaters, we watched them staring out from behind barbed wire inside a newly liberated concentration camp. For most of the war, we had no idea those camps existed, although there were rumors. Now there were pictures—too many of them. And you were immediately sorry you were ever the slightest bit curious to see what supposedly civilized people were capable of doing to each other.

We had to get out of there. A light rain was falling, a lakeshore drizzle, and rather than fight for a cab and waste the money, we did a brisk walk south along State Street, until we decided to join the couples we saw entering the lobby of the Palmer House. There a hastily hand-painted placard proclaimed "Victory Dance" and pointed the way to the Grand Ballroom, where a few thousand of our closest friends were getting smashed on half-off cocktails as they danced themselves delirious to the local wannabe big band. They were playing "Jumpin' at the Savoy," and even though the stuffed-shirt Palmer House wasn't the Savoy, it wasn't too shabby, and discount alcohol was not to be passed up.

After more than a few rounds and cutting the rug to shreds, Zelta and I slow danced in the lowered lights to "Moonlight Serenade."

Would I ever feel any better than this? I doubted it.

"Know what I like about you?" I asked her as I pulled her hot body closer, which till then hadn't seemed physically possible. She cuddled closer to me, and if I hadn't known it before, I knew it then. We were inseparable.

"No, what?" she asked innocently, *my indulgent feeder of straight lines!*

"You can play like a guy. But you sure don't feel like one."

Remember this, men, and it is the wisest thing you will ever know: Learn to dance. Because dancing is a vertical expression of a horizontal desire. Do it well, do it masterfully, and you won't ever have to sweat how well you know how to do the other. You'll be given plenty of chances to learn.

"I feel like a million bucks," Zelta moaned. "Ever notice how people handle money with so much...love? All those warm hands."

She had a point. She definitely had a point. The thought of money had got her thinking about sex, and that was all well and good, but the thought of money, and lots of it, just then seemed to me like a totally new idea.

"People are going to make fortunes after this war," I said, as if she should care. "Everybody needs everything!"

She nuzzled me, a little annoyed, I think, that I wasn't picking up on her passionate mood.

"Your father hates me," she said.

"Aw," I consoled her, "he just wants you to like him. He wants everybody to like him."

A wave of dizziness must have overtaken her as she slurred more than usual, "Wenzeeeee gebback?"

I wasn't at all sure.

"Soon as he settles the war in the Pacific," I said.

એ

Meanwhile in Rio de Janeiro, I was to learn, Milton and a few other bewildered passengers were descending the boarding stairs of a commercial DC-3. It was an unscheduled stop, and despite the welcoming clime this time of year, all of them had expected to be somewhere else.

Greeting them at the bottom of the gangway was a military policeman with a clipboard. As Milt stepped down to his eye level, the MP demanded, "Name?"

"Reynolds. Milton Reynolds. Say, what is this?"

"Sorry, pal," the MP drawled in mock commiseration. "We got orders to bump all civilians. They need these planes to take the rest of the shooting match to the Pacific."

Indeed, the War Department was wasting no time redeploying the forces in the European theatre to a war zone that was even more hostile and unfamiliar. The new venue was a muggy, slimy, creature-infested place in which none of the newly transferred troops had been trained to fight. It was a place where you were surrounded and nearly smothered by the dense jungle greenery, where snipers could be hiding anywhere, not just in the windows of some abandoned building you could not mistake for anything but a potentially enemy-infested hiding place.

"I've got to be in Chicago," Milton announced. And he did. There would be no time to waste trying to figure out how to circumvent the Biro patent and beat Eversharp to that huge pot of postwar gold.

"You're in Rio," the MP huffed. "Take a load off." As if rum, cheap cigars, and gorgeous hookers should be enough to satisfy any man.

Milt reached into his pocket and pulled out an ordinary wood pencil. He was a magician with the contents of that coat. He tapped the MP on the shoulder with it as he drew him aside.

"You'd deprive the war effort of this?" He held the pencil up, a device to be marveled at, no less than the pen. "It's military priority."

"We got pencils, Mac."

"This is a wood sample—disguised, of course—from the Argentine outback. Lighter than balsa wood, stronger than steel."

"Looks like a pencil," the guy said, unnecessarily. Fortunately, he did not challenge Milt's assertion and try to snap it in two. But then he didn't need to. Spotting pompous fools was more or less his job.

Milt was just warming up. "A fighter plane made out of this could —"

"Do skywriting?" The man loved his own sense of humor.

Milt was undeterred. In a hush, he confided, "This wood also grows in Japan."

The guy chuckled. "Hey, y'know, maybe they can work this shit out with a pencil. Get it?"

He gave Milt a slap on the back and turned back to his job of checking off the passenger list.

"A weisenheimer," he muttered, but he pocketed Milt's pencil.

Milt was furious. "I demand to see the priority officer."

ॐ

Maj. Brad Bilious (actually, I have no idea what his name was) sat at his desk in a Quonset hut just off the tarmac at the commercial airport in Rio. On this day in early May, it was unseasonably hot and muggy outside (at least, exceptionally uncomfortable by Chicago standards, which in the summer is no better). Inside it was a steam bath, and all he had was an ancient ten-inch rotary fan that spun so slowly you could see the blades. He'd draped the coat of his uniform over the back of his chair, but he didn't dare loosen his khaki tie. He'd long-since sweated totally through the pits of his dress twill shirt, but regulations are regulations, and you never knew when the brass would come charging through the door.

And here came Milton Reynolds—a civilian, no less, and without an escort. You'd have to be the kind of guy who is used to being in an important hurry to act like brass when you held no rank whatsoever.

The major had already been briefed on the guy. *We're not total idiots,* he reassured himself. What else was there to do besides shuffle requisitions and discourage over-zealous taxpayers?

"You the guy with the magic wand?" the major asked him, not looking up from signing reqs with his dime-store fountain pen.

"Milton Reynolds, Chicago. Is there no way —?"

Bilious cut him off with a look. God's girlfriend couldn't fly today. The officer obviously had paperwork to deal with, and in wartime you're either using up ammunition or you're using up paper. Much better for the sake of your health to be killing trees and asking no questions.

Now, the history of the Free World might have been different if this Bilious fellow had had a different hobby. But there smack on his desk was a dandy little item that did not, indeed could not, escape Milton's attention. It was the model of a classic single-engine high-wing monoplane of a type used by the Army as a trainer. Milt knew it well.

"Why, that's a Stinson Reliant!"

Bilious's official mask dropped in an instant and suddenly he was all smiles. "You a model builder?"

"Nossir," Milt cooed, helping himself to a chair. "I used to own one of those."

This guy was some big cheese, no mistake!

"Why, I trained in one," the major beamed, eyeing it lovingly. "A lot of us did. Best time of my young life, I must say. You know, barnstorming they call it but of course we weren't allowed much solo time and it's not like we could go dive-bombing sheep. But what a helluva lot of fun. I always wondered what it would be like to take your best girl up in one, and of course that was against the rules, as well. But on a clear day…" he sighed. "I don't have to tell you what a thrill it was."

"Oh, I envy you flyboys," Milt said, getting cranked up. "I had to hire me a pilot. Roger Q. Williams, maybe you heard of him? My eyes are so bad I shouldn't cross the street. But yes, of course, I love to fly. Nothing better."

(In fact, his eyes weren't all that bad, even though he was never seen without his wire-rimmed spectacles. But without the eyesight excuse, the major might think less of Milt's not going for a pilot's license himself.)

Williams had been the first to fly from New York to Rome, not long after Lindbergh's pioneering flight from St. Louis to Paris. Bilious had heard the name, even if he didn't know exactly what the guy had done, and was suitably impressed.

"You must've had some dough in those days," he observed. "Was it before the war? Did you have to give it up?"

"That plane was one helluva sales tool. Paid for itself," Milt bragged. "And, yes, regrettably, eventually I had to sell it when the business did a nose-dive. But in the glory days I sold printing equipment to retailers. My plane had four seats—you could order it with four or five, you know. So we could take a passenger or two and still have room for our luggage and sample cases. I never met a customer who could resist an invitation to take a spin. And these were all department-store executives. You know," although the major didn't but could imagine, "prep-school dandies in their pinstripe suits."

Milt grasped the model, and it was a measure of how enthralled his listener was that the guy didn't balk at this stranger manhandling his precious, delicately crafted toy.

Milt waved the thing dramatically in the air, banking expert turns as he emphasized its slow ascent, ever higher, until he had it hovering over the major's head.

"We'd take our time getting to altitude," Milt explained, "and then Williams knew to start circling. We'd pick some landmark, you know. Oo-ah! We'd be out over Lake Michigan and, 'Hey, get a load of the sailboat. And those girls on the deck in their halter tops!' And then before the guy could catch his breath, I'd ask for the order!"

Not being a salesman, the major probably didn't understand where this was going, so Milt helped him, "And that's when I tell him we'll land when he signs—or we run outta gas! I say it like a joke, see. But they all know I'm a little bit crazy. Who would take a chance?"

Finally both getting the joke and realizing his guest might be capable of just about anything, Bilious gave Milt a comradely slap on the back. For his part, Milt knew he'd closed another sale.

∽

Later that day, out on the tarmac a commercial TWA Constellation was boarding. The same MP stood faithfully by the stairs, checking passengers off a list on his clipboard. Most of them were either officers with military priority or enlisted men, including some ambulatory wounded who were being rotated home.

And here came an admiral, dressed to the nines in his whites.

The MP snapped to attention and gave a crisp salute before he realized he knew the guy, the guy who could apparently cure constipation with a pencil.

"You must have some pull," the MP said to him. Evidently he recognized the uniform. "The guy's body is still warm. His mother didn't tell him to wait for an hour before, er, swimming."

"Carry on corporal," Milt said cheerily as he saluted back and trotted up the stairs.

"Smooth sailing, Admiral." Never mind he was a sergeant, and very probably at that point he muttered something like, "Takes all kinds to win a war."

❧

Now, Milt told this get-out-of-jail-free story time and again over the years, and as with many of his recollections, often with considerable variation as to salient facts. In the case of Maj. Bilious (the name is my invention, not Milt's), the air-ace camaraderie makes a great story. But for the record (as if anyone cared about history), an alternate version is more mundane and perhaps more plausible in its method, but highly suspect as to how much it depends on a whopping coincidence.

In this version, when Milt asked, "...Is there no way?" the major shot back, "Not if you went to school with God."

So then, rising to the challenge, Milt wanted to know, "If you don't mind my asking, whose operation is this?"

And the major replied matter-of-factly, "My boss is Col. Jerome Waterman."

That's when you'd start to smell smoke, because right away, Milt asked, "Jerry Waterman? From Miami?"

And the startled guy said, "Come to think of it."

"He used to buy for Maas Brothers?"

You see, it's not at all incredible that Milt would know retailers, for reasons just explained. He did peddle sign-printing equipment and he did pretty much know all of the buyers and most of the executives. At the time, Maas Brothers was a well-known retail chain in the Southeast. So Milt was dropping a name he knew, that much we can grant him for being truthful.

Waterman was also the name of one of the long-established fountain-pen companies. That outfit figures into my story much later, but fortunately for the sake of not straining Milt's credibility any further, Jerry Waterman had no particular connection to pens unless he had one in his pocket.

"Seems he worked for some store," Bilious admitted.

"I didn't go to school with him," Milt said, "But I've bought him a thick steak or two. Jerry can verify my priority status."

So the skeptical officer handed Milt a telegram message pad and let him write whatever query he wanted to send the colonel.

"U.S. citizen's got a right to send a wire," he said. Then he handed Milt his own pencil. "Here, you can have it back. I don't want to know where it's been."

Sometimes that line would get a laugh, if Milt's listeners had been paying enough attention to connect the pencil with the MP's put-down. It would be doubly funny because latrine humor seldom fails, and this time Milt was the butt of his own joke.

That's one reason Milt would switch versions—if his punch line hadn't gotten a laugh last time around.

In another version of the story, as Milt told it, he simply called up the president of Eastern Airlines, who happened to be his old drinking buddy Eddie Rickenbacker, the former World War I flying ace. True or not, it was only the beginning of his rubbing elbows and getting into trouble with famous pilots.

7

The executive offices of Eversharp in New York City were beyond sumptuous. A popular advertising slogan of the time was, "A title on the door means a Karastan on the floor," referring to a premium brand of carpeting. In his richly appointed art-deco office, at an enormous teakwood desk that floated on a sea of the plush stuff, sat Martin Straus, a sleek heavy-hitter in the Madison Avenue marketing game. His taste ran to silk suits at a time when his conservative peers were proud of their stuffy worsted wool. His shirts were custom-made, starched-linen broadcloth, and his silk ties were the finest Italian. His silver hair and clipped mustache were barbered weekly at his desk, at the same time he received a meticulous manicure from a comely technician.

He was a man not to be underestimated, a competitor who relentlessly took advantage, a demanding boss who abhorred the word *no*.

On this particularly momentous day in the midst of wartime, Straus was surrounded by his faithful lieutenants. They'd been sweating bullets for weeks, and today the boss would finally get sight of their idea.

As Straus rose ominously from his desk, he brandished the company's current flagship product—a gleaming black *fountain* pen.

"Gentlemen," he pronounced, "the fountain pen is dead. Long live Odd-Ball Biro's little brainstorm!" And from his inside coat pocket he produced a shiny prototype. "The exclusive, patented *ballpoint*—from Eversharp!" And he waved it in front of their faces as if to hypnotize them with its magic.

Apparently, everybody in the small but growing revolutionary pen movement knew of "Odd-Ball," and very probably Biro's promoters had stuck poor László with the nickname because it was so memorable. As to the brand name Eversharp, no one took issue with the idea that a ballpoint was not at all sharp and hence didn't need to stay that way. Neither did a fountain pen, for that matter. The product name derived from disposable razor blades, and in that context, it made perfect sense. But as Straus and his cohorts well knew, you might throw away the blades, but you'd never abandon a brand name that had earned its popularity.

"Now!" Straus growled as he planted his palms on the desk and leaned forward to stare them down. "Where's my battle plan?"

One of the lieutenants—a skinny one in a cheap wool suit (we'll call him Smith)—jumped up. He walked over nervously to a drape-covered flipchart. And with a pleading look for encouragement from his fellows, he pulled the drape aside to reveal a colorful poster. The predominant theme was red-and-green Yuletide. A rosy-cheeked Santa was adjusting his spectacles to read a huge scroll. And in one mitten he held an oversized rendering of the miracle pen.

"Santa's making his list," Smith recited from the printed slogan, "and checking it twice—with his new Eversharp ballpoint pen!"

Straus sat slowly back into his leather chair. He rested his chin on his hand and stared for a long moment at the poster. Smith didn't dare move, nor did any of the others, much less did anyone venture to say anything. Silence descended on them like a pall, and the only discernible sound was the delicate ticking of the ormolu clock on Straus's desk.

Was it measuring out the final seconds of their gainful employment?

In fact, Straus was not particularly taken with this concept. For his personal taste, he would have preferred a pretty girl posed provocatively with the new thing. His prospects would be men, after all—returning vets, officers probably, who would be resuming their paper-pushing, white-collar jobs. And, for all the changes that had been wrought in the country in just a few years, prudishness was now old hat. The GIs had seen the seamy side of life, and these days a man could even tell a risqué joke in mixed company. Billboards teased them with exposed gams. And there were no more flat-chested movie stars. Breasts had swollen up to fill those blouses and sometimes even spilled out.

But, trying his ideas out on his wife the previous evening, he had stood corrected.

Yes, the pens would be for the men, as Christmas gifts. A good fountain pen cost five dollars, and there was no reason to offer these little gems at a lesser price. It was luxury goods, and there wouldn't be much of that to go around this season.

But it would be the woman who would do the shopping. It would be her big gift to him.

Straus had to admit, his wife was right. The consumers of his new product would be men, but its purchasers would be women—at Christmastime. And with any luck, the war would be over, or as good as over, and the household might have some money to spend.

For all its flash as a luxury item, the gift was practical. The wife or girlfriend would want credit for giving him what he'd no doubt show off as a status symbol around the office. But she'd justify it to herself thinking it was practical. Women make shopping lists. Businessmen make to-do lists. This pen is just the thing to make your list, and add to your gift list, and that's just what Santa here is doing.

"By God, I like it." Straus finally said in a low voice.

The room was suddenly abuzz with self-congratulation. Smith in particular was stunned. It was not lost on him that his selection from among his peers as spokesperson in all probability indicated a certain lack of confidence. If one of them had to stick his head out of the foxhole and get shot, it would be he. He had the least seniority, and he had no family.

But today he was a winner. Flushed with pride, his head bobbed in acknowledgement to Straus as he meekly resumed his seat.

Straus rose again. Naming his biggest competitor, he thundered, "Those poor bastards at Parker are going to drown in their own red ink!"

He laughed until he wheezed, and so did his good-natured fellows.

He grew steely-eyed and clenched his jaw, signaling his forthcoming charge to them in all seriousness.

"I want the rollout in October. We're going to hit them with everything we've got."

There was an audible, collective gasp among the troops. It was almost summer already. There was no time! Certainly, Straus wouldn't be setting the target unless manufacturing could deliver. But advertising campaigns took time to set up. This poster was just a notional thing. Every one of them had assumed the rollout would be Christmas season *after next*.

And ordinarily, retailers bought for Christmas no later than July. But this year was no ordinary year. For one thing, there were precious few consumer goods, not for lack of products but due to shortages of materials. For another, there were all kinds of rumors that peace would break out suddenly, perhaps any time, and no one in retailing was prepared.

But Straus seemed undeterred. "Men," he snarled, "this is top secret until *V-E Day!*"

Now, for the briefest moment, they feared he'd lost his grip. Victory in Europe had already been achieved—last month, in May. Did he mean the *anniversary* of V-E Day *next* year? But how did that square with the October launch?

Perhaps not surprisingly, not one of them asked for clarification.

Amused by their perplexity, Straus came around the desk. He dealt Smith a sound thwack on the back as he exclaimed, "Victory for *Eversharp!*"

He was still cackling with glee as Smith took up the poster and they all backed out of the room.

8

Milt returned to Chicago from Rio by way of three connecting flights and two layovers. But he did get home, when most civilians lacking military priority or innovative war materiel or friends in high places were still cooling their heels in distant ports waiting for the Pacific airlift to wind down.

Let's get a fix here. At this point, Milt had no idea how to make a ballpoint pen. He knew that stealing or otherwise infringing on Biro's patent was a bad idea, especially considering the corporate clout of the other big players in the game. These were sure to be the established fountain-pen manufacturers—namely, Parker, Waterman, Schaeffer, and Eversharp.

But could those fat-cat companies move fast enough? Like Straus, Milt's gut told him Christmas was the opportunity to be seized. But so far, all he had in has bag of tricks was a boatload of last season's Mexican cigarette lighters with see-through plastic fuel tanks.

None of that stopped him. Doing the impossible was his personal métier. According to him, whatever it was and no matter what the obstacle, you just went ahead and did it.

Meaning, without thinking. Without weighing the consequences. Actually, without applying anything like logical reasoning.

And he most certainly was not one for waiting while he solicited advice. Which is why his calling a family meeting seemed oddly out of character.

He hadn't been home but a couple of days, scarcely long enough to get a rest and check in at his office. (He was still running Printasign, from which issued the cash flow that floated our boat.)

Of course, Zelta and I were still houseguests who had overstayed. We were itching to get out, but the right time had yet to present itself. And besides, we had nowhere in particular to go. But we were going stir-crazy at the apartment, which was bad enough during the too-quiet dinners with Mom, but now that he was home, we knew it was just a matter of time before our nerves would fray to the breaking point.

Milt had spent his first full day at the office, and when he got home he announced we were all going to dinner. My mother's favorite place to dine out was the Ravisloe Country Club on the North Shore. She liked it because she could dress up in her newest frock, almost certain to be spotted by a gossipy someone from her social set.

So the four of us took his big Buick up Lake Shore Drive to the club in Evanston, where we were treated to a lavish meal that was memorable for several reasons. First off, it was lobster night. There were times during the war when you'd feel lucky to score a can of Spam, but these well-heeled members had no qualms about having their jumbo crustaceans flown in from Maine. Secondly, this particular delicacy necessitated the wearing of bibs to protect shirt fronts, ties, and décolleté cleavage from greasy drips of drawn butter. So we all looked equally foolish, and our costuming added to the party atmosphere.

The topics of dinner conversation that night alternated between the novelty of the delicious lobster and the perils of Milt's return trip. (This time we got the Jerry Waterman version of the story.) From Milt's terse remarks on returning from the airport, we already had a general idea that he'd met with Biro and come up dry. We had yet to learn he was more committed than ever to producing a pen.

We topped off the meal with cheesecake and coffee. Typically at this point, if Milt were feeling expansive and especially after a successful selling trip, he'd suggest we indulge in a brandy. But this time, he grew quiet, took a deep breath, and pulled Biro's pen dramatically from his coat pocket. I noticed right away it wasn't the Myles version he'd already swiped from Joel Goldblatt. He must have copped this Birome from Biro himself.

(Swiping pens was both a talent of his and a dumb stunt that would eventually catch up to us.)

Once he was sure all eyes were on him, he passed it ceremoniously to me. "What do you make of it, Jim?"

I fondled it. It didn't look all that special, and to anyone who didn't know its history and without close inspection, they couldn't tell it from an ordinary fountain pen.

"Go ahead," Milt nodded. "Take it apart."

So I disassembled the thing as carefully as I could, since I didn't want any pieces of the cherished thing to snap in my inexperienced hands. As I did so, Milt told us how Biro had explained the basis of his patent—capillary action—like sipping a soda through a straw.

"The capillary action is really ingenious," I observed. "He made the ink thick and gooey so it flows just enough but the thing won't leak. Nice. Very nice."

Mother chimed in, "People will like that. Fountain pens are so messy."

Milt stared across the table at me as if he were a heavy hitter at the plate, defying the umpire's call. "There has to be a way around the patent," he fumed.

I gave it serious consideration, but of course I didn't think it likely I'd be able to come up with a solution on the spot. Or anything that would be obviously better than what was surely a novel, perhaps a revolutionary, invention. "There has to be a way to get ink to the tip," I thought out loud.

The three of them looked at me expectantly, and I guessed Milt was asking himself whether the dough he'd sunk into my engineering degree wasn't entirely wasted. Even Zelta looked like she expected an answer, and a good one—if for no other reason than to show him I deserved to play in the big leagues.

"I don't know," I mused. "Some kind of plunger? Like a hypodermic?"

From the quick succession of Milt's facial expressions, I could tell he hadn't thought of that angle, didn't expect such a credible response from me. and ruled it out right away as impractical.

As if reading my mind, appeasing me, and making sure he'd grant me a passing grade, Mom said to him, "I always said he won't go wrong with a technical background."

I was thinking I might have actually whistled past the graveyard on this one. I didn't look like a total idiot.

So stating what I thought was the obvious in an attempt to lighten the moment with a joke, I said, "Too bad you can't patent the law of gravity."

Often the one to top my punch lines, Zelta teased, "And who invented the wheel? I bet somebody shot her on the way to the patent office."

Milton looked at her in earnest. "Is that true?"

Zelta was sure he was pulling her leg. "That a woman invented the wheel? Heck, yes!"

He was still dead serious. "No, that you can't patent the law of gravity."

Realizing the question could have just as well been directed to me, I responded, "In fact you can't patent any naturally occurring process."

"You don't say," Milt said, almost to himself.

I was sure he understood this part, but for the benefit of all concerned, I was quick to add, "So what? Without a patent, you have no way to hold off the competition."

"We just have to be first," he said. "If you're going to do the impossible, you have to do it right away."

Uh-oh, that tired line.

"Yeah, well," I tried to get him to see, "for starters you'd have to make the ink a lot thinner."

And contrary to Milt's spirit of unfounded optimism but reinforcing me, Zelta chuckled, "Then the thing would leak like a stuck pig."

Ignoring all of this, Milt raised his glass, which at this point held only water. "Eureka! Ladies and gentlemen, to the Big Idea—the Reynolds Pen!"

None of us could know then, but Zelta's words were prophetic, and so was toasting to its success—with water.

So, he'd found it. Or rather, we'd found it. Or I'd sold it and he'd bought it. Or I tossed it to him and he'd run with it. The Big Idea. From that moment, I was hooked. After all, wasn't it, in a sense, my idea? Actually, no—it was a force of Nature!

He looked at me and he was as happy as he'd ever been. "We'll use gravity! We'll steal it fair and square!"

Could capillary action move mountains? Or keep the whole universe from flying apart?

We had the force of gravity on our side!

Not long after the lobster incident, Zelta and I got our own place in Chicago. She did the scouting and found it, we both went to have a look, and I blessed her choice. With the war's winding down, demand was up and there weren't many apartments to pick from. It was a one-bedroom walk-up in Lincoln Park, on the other side of downtown from Edna and Milt. It would be close enough for me to commute by city bus to Milt's places of business, but far enough away we could mind our own business, should we ever find the time.

Why did she agree to stay? After he'd made the decision to go for the pen, it seemed we'd signed on for the duration. Zelta and I never got around to expressing reasons or reservations to each other. Probably it was mostly about wanting to move out and finally having a place we could call home. Milt had offered me a job (without being specific about either the job description or the pay), and that pretty much decided it. We thought we could afford an apartment, so we got one and drew the line on Mom's trying to furnish it for us, although Zelta did permit her to hang curtains.

I knew Zelta wasn't hooked and didn't feel obligated to stay.

Maybe she was just curious.

For his part, Milt hired a "real" engineer, rented a machine shop, and we were soon cooking with gas. The geeky little guy's name was Orville, and he was not only proficient in mechanical design but he also was an accomplished hands-on machinist. (Now, Chicago is notoriously a union town, and normally one man wouldn't be able to do both jobs. But fortunately, no one was paying attention, even though at war's end the business community was being pressured to create as many jobs as possible.)

Milt described to the two of us what he had in mind. I made sketches, and Orville ran off the prototypes. He turned the pen barrels on a lathe from war-surplus aluminum tubing. And somehow he figured out how to modify watch-making machinery to mill the brass tip that held the stainless-steel ball. The clearance between the tip opening and the ball had to be precise, as well as uniform from one pen to the next. Too tight, and the ball would freeze up or not turn at all. Too loose, and the ball would fall out as ink leaked out around it. Very quickly, we didn't bother with formal drawings because no sooner would we get it down with some precision on paper than we'd have Orville trimming or tweaking or otherwise modifying the part.

I tested the pens, while Milt handled what you'd call the forward planning. This involved securing financing (which may have had to do with juggling the accounts at the printing-equipment warehouse), talking to potential and unnamed business partners who never materialized, and conferring with his "executive staff." Those guys were the managers at Printasign and included nobody new. Their role seemed pretty much to listen and nod. But he was always having meetings with them. Then he'd drop around to the machine shop, take a quick look at my latest batch of failures, make some terse comments about how this or that might be different, and leave admonishing us to keep up the good work, fretting about how little time we had, and promising to check back soon.

Then began what I'd call our "messy period."

Sometimes the little ball bearing would freeze up and the thing wouldn't write at all.

Or, the ball fell out and ink drained freely from the pen, all over the paper, and if you didn't stanch the flow quickly enough, over the side of the desk and onto my lap. After I ruined one pair of pants, I bought some surplus coveralls, even though Milt expected proper business attire at all times and himself never so much as loosened his tie. Orville wore a shop coat, one he must have had at a former place of employment because it had his name stitched on a little patch above the breast pocket, where predictably he carried his pencils and a trusty fountain pen. (For the record, he had an Eversharp Wahl fountain pen and pencil set, which dated from the 1920s. The set was solid gold and sold for the whopping price of a hundred and twenty-five dollars. I think it's safe to say Orville was a pen fancier, which perhaps explains his dedication and, not least important, his patience.)

We could crank out two or three prototypes a day, depending on whether we could modify a previous design or needed to start from scratch. Orville had gathered various widths and thicknesses of aluminum tubing as well as some solid bar stock. The ball bearings were various "found objects" from household items, such as children's toys.

After a couple of dozen unsuccessful attempts, it was almost September, and we didn't think we were any closer to a solution. That's when Orville walked in one morning and declared it had come to him in the shower. Our main problem, he said, was the lack of fine precision in the ball bearings. So while he worked on the next-generation pen barrel, he gave me the assignment of finding a source for one-millimeter ball bearings. He'd heard they use them in aircraft bombsights.

I looked through trade magazines and catalogues at the public library, and I phoned around. Finally a Stanford buddy who'd taken a job with Douglas Aircraft in Santa Monica said he thought SKF made them. This Swedish company was known for its precision bearings, and although their products were in all kinds of U.S.-made munitions, they'd taken some heat over here because they were also supplying the Germans.

When I got a U.S.-based SKF sales rep on the phone, he was eager do a deal. I shouldn't have been so surprised. How many bombsights does an aircraft have? One? That would be exactly one ball bearing per sight, per expensive plane. And military aircraft manufacturing had all but stopped except for replacement parts.

When I told the guy I wanted a hundred thousand of them, he made me repeat myself.

The order would fit into a bucket about the size of a gallon paint can. He'd send them in an air courier pouch the next morning, and I could cab over to Meigs Field and pick them up as easily as a batch of fluff-and-fold.

Oh, and the price? I could take them on approval, he said. They were, after all, war surplus.

But then he got curious and asked what they were for. And not wanting him to go knocking on any competitors' doors, I told him we were retooling a munitions plant to make toy puzzles, sort of like a pocket-sized pinball machine. He thought it was a neat idea, and I remember thinking if pen manufacturing went bust, the puzzle thing could be a butt-saver.

The next morning when I returned to the shop from the airfield with my prize, I couldn't wait to show Orville. I didn't expect to find Milt there, but apparently there were no secrets from him, and he was just as excited to catch sight of the bombsight balls.

I was so excited, I pried open the lid with too much force, and thousands of little ball bearings spilled out, all over the floor. Milt's first instinct was to grab the bucket away from me, but as he rushed over, bearings on the floor got under the soles of his wingtips, and he went ass-over-teakettle, landing square on his ample, wool-pinstriped keister. Said ignominious downfall would have been disastrous enough had he not on the way down also grabbed desperately onto a wire shelving unit that held several cans of our samples of gelatinous printers' inks, in varying viscosities.

It took all of the night and a good part of the next day for me to get the place clean, including sweeping up the errant ball bearings and washing them with solvent and then distilled water in a sieve so they'd be usable should Orville's hunch prove correct. And I had to reorder most of the ink.

It took me considerably longer to live down Milt's disapproval, which was only partially assuaged by my diligent efforts to make the shop shipshape. I wasn't let out of the doghouse until later, but not all that much later, for reasons having to do with the next unfortunate episode.

You would think, by virtue of lessons learned, that would have been the end of our messy period. But it wasn't, not by a long shot.

Milt had a growing sense, as I did, that the precision bearings were the key—even before we were able to prove as much with a working prototype. But he was already thinking ahead to the next big challenge—how to manage mass production. It would do us no good to be able to turn out few finely crafted, handmade pens. We had to be able to produce thousands in a day and with little enough labor so that our cost would be just pennies more than the expense for raw materials. The price of the pen had to be high but reasonable—something an upscale consumer could afford—while preserving a margin that, we hoped, would make us rich beyond the dreams of avarice.

Orville cautioned that the main barrier to achieving high-volume production would be filling each barrel with ink. That's when he happened on his idea for a "centrifugal filling machine."

Now he was dividing his time between making prototype pens and building his machine. Empty pen barrels stuck out from a hollow wheel like spokes. It held a reservoir of ink at the center. As the horizontally mounted wheel spun, ink would be forced out from the center, into the hollow wheel, and from there through gasketed holes and into the pens.

With the benefit of hindsight, we should have tested the filling machine at a slower speed, with only a small supply of ink, and not in front of an audience.

Milt had already told Mom and Zelta we had a working pen, which was not quite true. One afternoon he invited them over to the shop to see the "next Big Idea," by which we'd soon be producing the miracle pens by the carload.

The women were dressed up for downtown and depart-ment-store shopping. As the four of us watched, Orville flipped the switch on the electric motor, and the filling machine began to spin. Like a ceiling fan with big, heavy blades, it took several seconds to get up to speed. But very quickly it was whirring with a marvelous hum—the hum, we were sure, of successful capitalist enterprise.

That's when the clip that held one of the pens to the wheel sprang loose, the pen popped out of its seal, and the whirling-dervish machine flung big gobs of ink all over the walls—and us.

Not a person was spared.

The ladies wanted to research solvents that would get the stains out of their nice clothes. Milt wouldn't hear of it and told them to discard the dresses. Orville would have to buy them new ones out of his paycheck.

With hindsight, we'd have been much better off later if we'd let them investigate.

Thus did Orville usurp my place of honor in the doghouse. And after he mended the machine and his slipshod ways, *that* was the end of our messy period.

෴

It was September 1, 1945, a bleak night in old Chi-town, and it was pouring rain. Typically, this time of year was end-of-summer hot and muggy, but here it was downright chilly. The wind off the lake was brisk and drove the rain into your face like stinging spit. Mother Nature was not showing her friendly side.

Or so I would soon find out because I'd spent the day and most of the night inside the shop with Orville, as we fretted over what we hoped would be our final-final version of the Reynolds Pen.

I'd phoned Zelta earlier to tell her not to wait up, and she must have called Mom to let her know and maybe complain a bit. The long hours and late nights were wearing all of us down. She'd offered to bring food, but I told her I'd just grab a sandwich from the diner, which I didn't get around to doing, of course.

Milt dropped by about ten that night, at which point we had nothing to show. So he hung up his coat, plunked himself down at his makeshift desk in the corner, and actually loosened his tie. No sooner had he sat down in the chair and folded his hands on his tummy than he was in a deep, snoring sleep. Fine, he wouldn't be pestering us every five minutes.

The clock on the wall behind him read 1:24 in the early hours of September 2 when I nudged him awake. "Hey, hey. You said you wanted to see it."

Milt grabbed the prototype, squinting at it in the dim light. "Yeah? What's different?"

"We had to make the ink even thinner, which means the barrel has to be bigger to hold more or it would always need refilling."

Our pen was a fat boy. What else could you do?

He didn't even take time to root around for a scrap of paper. He quickly signed the blotter on his desk, "Milton Reynolds," with a flourish. The writing was thick, bold, and very wet.

"It's perfect!" he pronounced.

"Maybe not —"

"No, it's *perfect,*" he insisted. "We made it bigger so that it will never run out of ink!"

I shot him my "don't give me that same old crap about the video lighter" look.

"Well," he demurred, "not for a long, long time."

"It's not perfect," I said. "Maybe closer, but not what anybody would call perfect."

"It's September already. If it writes, I can sell it. If we miss the Christmas rush, we might as well go back to selling video lighters. Where's Orville?"

I stifled a yawn. "I sent him home."

Milt jumped up, grabbed his coat, and threw his arm around me. "Come on, kid. I'll buy you a drink."

&

Outside, we stepped into the downpour. Pulling his suit jacket over his head, Milt yelled, "Let's run for it!"

Our friendly neighborhood establishment was just over on the next block in an industrial area that was mostly warehouses and a meat packing plant.

As we passed under a streetlamp, my eye caught something that stopped me in my tracks.

Behind the glass in the newspaper vending machine was the big headline, "War's Over!"

We were getting drenched, but we just stood and stared. The Japanese had surrendered a couple of weeks ago, but nobody was ready to believe it was over until the Emperor signed the peace treaty.

Milt dug into his pocket for change and bought a copy and quickly tucked it under his arm.

He was all sincerity when he said, "Now we got another reason to celebrate."

He threw his arm around me again, and we minded not at all that we were soaked to the skin.

そ

Our local joint was Lulu's Bar and Grill, and there was Lulu behind the bar, a veteran of the trade who still had her looks.

"Where you boys been?" she asked as she continually polished the already gleaming bar. "The rest of the gang took off for downtown. It may be pouring, but I bet they're dancing in the street."

She didn't expect an answer and of course by now we knew what everyone else in the world knew.

"Black coffee for me," Milt commanded, "and a double whiskey for my grandfather here." I was surprised he didn't want a drink, but I suppose by now he was pumped and didn't want to take the edge off. He wouldn't get any sleep at all that night, I bet. Pen or no pen, I was ready to pack it in.

Milt spread the newspaper out on her clean bar. Even though he'd kept it folded and tucked, it was pretty soggy.

Then he pulled out the pen.

Lulu glared at him. "Milton, if that one leaks, you're out of here."

"Do you know what you're looking at?" And he held it up to her as if she hadn't witnessed the failure of dozens of our demonstrations.

"If I'm patient," she said, "I'm sure you'll tell me." (Milt was a good tipper, maybe that's why she cut him slack.)

He was already rehearsing his spiel. "This fantastic, miraculous, atomic-age pen won't run out of ink for two years!"

That was the windup, here was the pitch, and he was just getting up to speed.

"You can go to the remotest ice floe in the Aleutians where ink has never been heard of, stay for two whole years, and this veritable camel of a pen won't ask for a drink."

Never mind he was exaggerating shamelessly, not to mention his mixing of metaphors. But he was brilliant, and, like I say, he was just getting started. No wonder all he wanted was coffee.

"You don't have to ask at Lulu's, just kind of grunt," she said with her characteristic deadpan look. "Does this one write?"

She was obviously not one to succumb to flowery talk. She wanted to see your flowers and your box of candy, and even then she might not put out.

But Milt knew he almost had her. "It writes in the stratosphere at twenty thousand feet, and it writes on cloth, and..."

And for the big payoff, he wrote "Lulu" on the newspaper. On the *soaking-wet* newspaper!

"It writes under water," I said, reporting the obvious but not at all believing my eyes.

Milt did it again, this time scrawling all over the page. And wherever the pen touched, damp or moist or in a puddle, it left a bold, true line.

Milt, too, was amazed. "It writes *under water*."

For her part, Lulu was not particularly impressed. "Maybe I came in late. You making a thing for the Navy?"

I tried it. "Actually, it writes *even better* when the page is wet."

Never mind we'd ruined this collector's item front page with our doodles.

Or maybe we'd created one.

Milt was overjoyed and kept saying, "It writes under water. It writes under water…"

Lulu and I exchanged baffled looks. "I don't get it either," I said.

But Milt was way ahead of us. "Don't you see? It's part of the Big Idea. A new kind of pen so amazing, it writes under water. It's crazy. But people will wonder about it, they'll talk about it, and they'll make us—a *sensation*."

No denying, Milt had a sixth sense for coming up with sure-fire marketing gimmicks. You see, to my engineer's mind, the notion that the thing would write under water was totally impractical and therefore of no importance. But Milt was able to foresee that people would find the claim *outrageous*—not in the sense it was impossible, but that it was a ridiculous thing to boast about. And so they'd tell their friends this whopper, and those friends would tell their friends, and so on. Now, my academic training *did* extend to understanding the essence of mathematical geometric progression, and even though I was slow to catch on, I began to appreciate the power and the speed of word-of-mouth advertising.

Milt turned to me and grabbed me by both arms as if he were going to shake sense into me. But he just gripped firmly as he stated, "You and I are going on a sales call. To New York City!"

All I wanted was sleep.

❧

By mid-morning I'd managed to catch a few winks in my own bed, but I was up packing my bag. Other than a quick good-night kiss, I hadn't been able to explain to Zelta. Not that I knew much more than I had to be on a plane with him at noon.

"I haven't seen you do anything but brush your teeth and snore for the last two months," she fumed. "But suddenly it's hello I've got to go to New York?"

"He wants to make a pitch to Gimbels," I told her. "It's now or never."

She looked at me as if I'd just bought an acre of swampland or found Jesus at a prayer meeting. But she didn't give me an argument, and she insisted on riding with me to Midway, where I swallowed most of her lipstick in a whopper of a good-bye kiss.

10

n the waiting room outside Fred Gimbel's office on the executive floor of the Manhattan store, Milt was chatting up Dottie Moss. I got the feeling he and Gimbel's secretary had something of a history. But I suspected from the way she kept him at a distance that it stopped at flirtation.

As he resumed his seat by me, he said quietly, "Great guy, Fred Gimbel. Ladies man, smooth talker."

In fact, the Gimbels store chain advertised itself as, "Good old Gimbels, the plain store for plain people." Fred, I'd soon learn, was anything but plain. He was a class act. And his store was anything but lackluster.

"Are you going to tell him it leaks?" I asked, just as quietly.

"Are you kidding?" was all he said as he grinned his face off at Dottie.

The intercom on her desk buzzed, and she announced, "Mr. Fred will see you now."

જી

Fred Gimbel, the junior of the store-owner brothers, was as dapper and charming a man as you'd ever meet. Ivy League in three-piece tweeds. (At Stanford we used to call that a *four-piece* suit—jacket, pants, vest, and a zip-on flame.) And, most exceptional of all, he was a gentlemen among retailers, a coarse breed that delighted in grinding their vendors to a fine powder before they blew them away.

He was semi-reclined in his desk chair, legs crossed, the long pant legs hitched up far enough so his gartered argyle socks were showing.

He was holding the pen delicately between two fingers like a thermometer, as if he might actually be able to measure its sales potential.

"I don't know, Reynolds," he said without taking his eyes off it. "We can't give away those video lighters of yours."

Milt was on his feet, hovering, but careful not to crowd the guy. "Take this and I'll make the bad man go away."

Gimbel suddenly looked up at him. "Exclusive?"

Milt jumped on it. "Commit to twenty-five hundred units, you can have them for five fifty, and I never heard of Macy's."

Mr. Fred's cautious gaze returned to the pen. "I don't know. Eversharp is working on something like this." And he looked up again. "Got your bases covered, legal-wise?"

Milt always made his mistakes in a loud, clear voice. "They can't touch us. And I hear they're late. You better do it now if you want it for Christmas."

"Ours writes under water," I offered, realizing too late I was ad-libbing when Milt was a stickler for going by the script on sales calls.

"Whatever for?" Gimbel wanted to know.

"Theirs can't do that," I shot back, not exactly answering the question.

The intercom buzzed, and Gimbel pressed a button. Dottie's voice said, "Private on line two, sir."

He waved a finger at us to excuse himself and picked up the phone. As he did, Milt rushed over to me.

"Will you let me handle this?" he whispered.

"I was just—" was all I could manage to say.

We overheard Gimbel say, in a low voice, "Now, darling, I'm in a meeting…"

Gimbel held the receiver away from his ear and, although we couldn't hear what the angry female voice was saying, we could definitely tell it was female. And angry.

As the voice ranted on, he gently placed the phone back on the hook.

I don't know why he addressed his next remark directly to me, but perhaps because of my recent bachelor status he thought I would understand: "Why do they call them the fairer sex? Never known a one of them to fight fair."

He said it in all seriousness, but after a beat I realized it was his brand of dry humor, and I managed a knowing smile.

To Milt, he said, "I'm meeting Martin Straus for dinner at the Stork Club." Indicating the phone, he added, "And my date just canceled. Why don't you chaps come along?"

Gulp!

తు

Milt had never dealt with Straus, but he knew of him by reputation. And the reverse was true, not necessarily to Milt's credit, because Eversharp prided itself on its luxury gift items, which did not include video lighters.

On the plus side, we were on time to meet up with Fred, and Straus was running late. So we had a chance for a few drinks and some friendly chat before the inevitable confrontation.

After I'd had a couple, I told a story on myself, which in retrospect might have been unprofessional. But the senior men were sucking it down just as fast and seemed eager to hear. So I related how circumstances had forced me to pop the question to Zelta, and not the way I'd planned it. "So there he was," I said in my wind-up, "a complete stranger, bragging he was going to propose to my girl."

"My God," Gimbel commiserated. "Cheeky bastard. What did you do?"

"Let's just say I closed the deal before the competition could make his pitch."

Turning to Milt, Gimbel quipped, "Chip off the old blockhead, I'd say."

Gimbel was trying to signal the waiter for another round. I was about to tell them how I'd charged up to her in the dining hall, when suddenly here came Straus.

As he strode over to our table, Gimbel muttered, "Gentlemen, you're about to meet your Macy's."

We all stood to greet him as he shook hands with Fred, who made the introductions. "Martin Straus of Eversharp, meet Milton and James Reynolds of the Reynolds International Pen Company." Then without any prompting from us, and without resuming his seat, he handed our new pen to Straus, adding, "They call it a ballpoint."

Somewhat awkwardly, we all remained standing while Straus examined the shiny, aluminum pen. Then he handed it back, speaking only to Gimbel. "Fred, at the risk of embarrassing your guests, I'd say we have a case for patent infringement."

Lightly, I thought, and without rancor, Milt said, "Gravity feed, Straus. You got a patent on gravity?"

Still not looking directly at us, Straus replied, "Nonsense. They've stolen our design." Then he turned to Milt and shot back, "I've heard about you."

Milt smiled sweetly at him. "I'd give you one, but Fred here took all my samples!" Then he sat down and spread his hands as if indicating the lavish feast not yet laid out. "What's the matter? Lost your appetite?"

"I won't be dining with you," Straus snarled, "but I intend to eat your share." Then he said to Gimbel, "If you sell this thing, I'll pull every one of our products from your store. And that's for starters."

Gimbel looked unperturbed. He sat down and so did I. "Martin," he said, "I promise I won't do anything hasty. Now please do be sensible and have a drink."

But Straus abruptly excused himself, saying, "Gentle-men," spun on his heel, and left.

It took a moment for Milt to realize that, even though he judged he'd won this round with Straus, Gimbel had stopped short of a ringing endorsement. "Fred," he asked, "we've got a deal, don't we?"

Gimbel didn't answer but started to scan his menu intently. "I wonder what's good tonight? I'm famished."

❧

Once again, Milt was doing his best to make Dottie smile, but she was even cooler than before.

"Hey, Dottie, can we see your boss?"

"Sorry," she said. "Quote I have no time unquote. Weren't you headed back?"

"We, ah, missed our train," Milt fibbed. "Did he give us an order?"

All Dottie said was "He wired your office this morning, but I didn't see it. His Western Union pad is still on his desk."

Milt took this the wrong way, but he tried not to let her see his disappointment. "Thanks for dinner, Fred," he joked. "Have a nice life, guys!"

She looked genuinely apologetic. For all she knew, perhaps we had lost the sale. "He's so busy. Biggest

Christmas in years, all the boys coming home, but where's the merchandise?"

Out in the hallway as we waited for the elevator, Milt could no longer restrain his frustration.

"So, you thought you charmed him. Two guys from snob schools."

"He's a swell guy," I said, trying to sound positive.

"Swell," Milt fussed.

"Something the matter?" I wasn't sure of the situation, and I didn't see how he could be.

"Your new best friend didn't give us the order, young man!"

"Oh, it's my fault now?"

"You know what your problem is Mister College Boy?" And it was as upset as he'd been with me in a very long time. What he said next was a stab to the heart, especially coming from him. "You want to be liked more than you want the sale."

I actually wanted to cry, but I'm glad I didn't give him the satisfaction. "I'll call the office" was all I said.

"You do that," he called out as I walked away. "I'm going back in there."

ↄ⁀ↄ

Milt was teasing Dottie again, and maybe she was giving him a little more encouragement because she felt guilty that our sales trip had gone bust.

When I opened the door on them, I heard him ask her, "So, you got a favorite perfume?"

Only after she giggled and blushed did he look up to see me.

I was out of breath, having run up the stairs rather than wait for the elevator. Ernie, a staffer I'd recruited hastily from their sign department, stood right behind me holding his big press camera.

"He sent a wire," I panted.

"We knew that," Milt said dismissively.

I should have written it down, but I had it memorized: "Angry Straus good sign stop. Make that fifty thousand units stop. Gimbel."

Milt's forgiveness was immediate and unconditional, if not apologetic.

"This is Ernie," I said, catching my breath. "He's the store photographer."

"We're back in the game!" Milt shouted. He grabbed Ernie by the arm and headed straight for the door of Gimbel's office. "Shoot first and ask questions later."

Dottie was going to tell them he was too busy, but she couldn't get the words out fast enough.

In the private office, Milt thrust out his hand, used the grip to yank Gimbel out of his chair, and turned him to face front as Ernie closed in on them and they both grinned like apes.

Through his smile, Gimbel muttered, "Reynolds, please tell me I won't regret this."

And the flashbulb popped.

11

Our first plant was a converted tennis court just south of the Loop. So we were ready for a big success or a very expensive game of mixed doubles.

Our assembly lines were long cafeteria tables set with bins of small parts. We had about two dozen workers, including Mom and Zelta, who looked like older and younger versions of Rosie the Riveter in their standard-issue coveralls. You could say they got drafted.

"I like working with my hands" was the way Mom described it to Zelta. "Like knitting."

But as far as my wife was concerned, it was conscripted slave labor. Their task was to insert a little metal cap in the end of each barrel and tap it in place with a mallet.

Orville and I got new coveralls, as well, but ours were already grimy with ink as we wrestled with the filling machine to install a fresh set of gaskets. We couldn't afford the downtime from another snafu with the whirling dervish.

Milt stormed over to us, waving a newspaper. He was in a fresh shirt and tie. No dirty work for him.

"Full page of the Sunday Times," he said. "Gimbel went all out!" The pens were set to go on sale the next day at Gimbels' flagship store in Manhattan. So this was the *New York Times*. It would be a while before we hit the Chicago papers. I didn't know what a full-page ad cost, but I assumed it was not cheap.

Milt read from the ad: "'Two years without refilling. The pen you've read about, wondered about, waited for. It even writes under water.'" Milt beamed. "He bought the whole story! We're going to be big!"

"Isn't this nice," Mom observed, "the whole family, working together?"

"What if nobody buys them?" Zelta grumbled.

"What if they leak?" I couldn't help saying, but hoping I'd get some points at home for taking her side.

Mom thought a moment, then asked, "What if we can't make them fast enough?"

We all looked at her. It was a new thought.

☙

The day after the ad appeared was Monday, October 29, 1945. The morning in New York was cool and crisp. At the Thirty-second Street entrance of Gimbels, the sidewalk was thronged with excited shoppers. More were arriving by the minute, by bus and taxi and on foot, so many that they were spilling into the intersection, blocking traffic, and inspiring a chorus of angry car horns. Police estimates later put the eventual size of the crowd at five thousand. The air was filled not only with anticipation but also with diesel exhaust. But no one noticed or cared. These were New Yorkers.

The store windows were fully decked out for Christmas. Only days away, Halloween would be a non-event this year. They were all saving their money for the big holiday, looking forward to tearful family reunions, overstuffed feasts, and a heap of long overdue presents under the tree.

The retail price of the pen was set at twelve fifty. You could get an expensive hotel room for that. Because of wartime price controls, we actually had to get approval to have a price that high from the federal Office of Price Administration.

Milt had hoped they'd let him sell it for as much as ten bucks. The two-fifty was gravy, courtesy your Uncle Sam. (At that time, before it became much more inexpensive to make, materials and labor for each pen cost Milt eighty cents.)

I wasn't there—we were all back in Chicago furiously making pens—but I can imagine from the reports.

Two women, the mother Alma and her daughter Irma, were squeezed into the crowd. The store had yet to open, and the doors were locked. Some of the people were clutching twenty-dollar bills, holding them up at the ready but away from would-be snatchers. Impatient early arrivals jostled Irma as she struggled to count a wad of dollar bills she fished from her purse. Then she shoved forward as she tried to hand the money to Alma, who was closer to the door.

"Mom!" Irma called out. "If you get in first, get one for Hank!"

"Do I see Hank here?" Alma shot back. "It's every man for himself!"

A police paddy wagon pulled up, right up over the curb and onto the sidewalk. The crowd reluctantly gave way. Then another vehicle showed up and another and another, until there were five police wagons parked in a ring surrounding the door with fifty uniformed officers determined to keep these "plain folks" in line.

By this time, the crowd filled the intersection and traffic was gridlocked.

Officers O'Toole and Reilly shoved through the crowd brandishing their nightsticks and hoping the sight of their weapons would be enough to discourage pandemonium.

"Jeez," O'Toole said. "What've they got? Nylons?"

"Some pen writes under water" was Reilly's reply.

"Get outta here."

"They want twelve fifty," Reilly added knowingly. "Not on my salary."

O'Toole looked around and shook his head. "So this is it. Your postwar hysteria."

Inside the store, floorwalker Myron Sitkiewicz finished preparations by fastidiously brushing the lint from his morning coat. He wore a fresh boutonniere in his lapel and a paste-diamond stickpin in his gray satin ascot. He was ready for the biggest day of his career. Just behind him stood Fred Gimbel in his signature tweeds.

And on the other side of the door, just inches behind the glass, was the clamoring, assembled multitude. There was no hiding from them.

"Open up! Let's go! What's the holdup?" came the shouts, which Myron feared could get downright ugly if they waited any longer.

He and Gimbel looked around behind them to survey the floor one more time. The salesclerks were all standing at attention at their assigned positions behind the counters.

"All right," Gimbel said quietly to Myron. "Battle stations."

"Wha-what do I do now?" Myron asked him, as if he didn't know but perhaps was hoping at the last minute the raid had been canceled and he could return safely to his foxhole.

"Why, open the door" was Gimbel's firm order, "and stand back!"

In the blink of an eye, his boss disappeared and Myron was left to fend for himself. He said a silent prayer, turned the key in the lock, and the frenzied crowd rushed past him as he tried to make himself as thin as possible, squeezed up against a wall.

Crazed shoppers grabbed fistfuls of pens from baskets, waved their bills at the salesclerks, and even wrestled pens from each other.

They ignored everything else in the store except the counters where pens were spread out.

Exercising contingencies he'd never dreamed necessary, Myron had to send for reinforcements, directing idle clerks in other areas to come in and assist the harried pen sellers.

More than once, he personally carried a basketful of pens from a hidden cache in a janitorial closet. He held it high as people grabbed for their prizes, and he even elbowed a few who were so brazen as to try to knock the whole load out of his hands. But he made it across the field and handed it off to the first available clerk he found, a junior associate in lingerie.

The crazies lost all interest in him as she was beset by the swarm.

He used the moment to recover his composure. Catching sight of himself in a mirror, he saw his morning coat looked like he'd slept in it, his ascot was askew, and his ashen face was in shock.

He walked unsteadily over to the water cooler by the elevator. He was about to take a refreshing sip when its doors parted to reveal none other but Fred Gimbel. Seeing the bedlam, the normally reserved executive grinned like a little boy getting his first bicycle.

"Mr. Fred, Mr. Fred!" Myron appealed to him. "These people are animals. We've taken over umbrellas, knocked out clocks, and we're going into silver."

Together they surveyed the scene.

"Ballpoint pens all over the place," the floorwalker sighed.

Gimbel had a flash of inspiration. "My God, man, this is a department store. Tell them they have to buy something else to get a pen."

Before Myron could protest, the elevator door closed on Gimbel and he re-ascended.

"But they don't want anything else," Myron was left to say to himself.

လ

Before the day was out, Gimbel was not only enforcing his purchase-with-a-purchase policy, but he'd also decreed that, henceforth, his sales clerks had to use Reynolds pens exclusively to write up orders. And back in Chicago, we were loading more pens on an airplane for rush delivery to him. Reportedly, some individual shoppers bought pens by the dozen. (Did that mean they also had to buy a dozen brassieres?) The store sold ten thousand pens by closing time that Monday. The sales volume—in pens alone—was fully a third of their typical day's gross receipts.

And before the week was out, ballpoint pen mania was sweeping the country. The first postwar Christmas shopping season was ablaze, and Reynolds pens were fueling the fire. Milton's promises about the product had been hardly modest, but sellers everywhere didn't hesitate to repeat even the most grandiose claims. Not only would it write under water, it would work at high altitude, go two years without refilling, and never leak or skip. Because you could bear down on its tip without "splaying a nib," it would make up to eight carbon copies—a bureaucrat's dream come true!

And Fred Gimbel was not the only retailer who realized a purchase with a purchase could generate greater profits. Milt was already calculating that, even if the pen *did* go a couple of years before running dry, refilling it would require its return to the factory.

In an exclusive boutique, a lady would admire herself in a new evening gown in front of a full-length mirror. The salesclerk would suggest a shiny clutch-purse to set off the outfit. No sooner would the lady be admiring the way the purse looked with the dress than the clerk would add, "You know, a new pen would coordinate nicely with that purse."

At gas stations all over the country, the pump jockey would lean in as you drove up, give you a big smile, and ask, "Fill 'er up? Want a pen?"

Or at a barber shop: "Six bits for the haircut. Want a pen with that?"

At a jewelry store: "Silver cuff links? I think we have a matching pen."

And, I wasn't sure, but before long I bet there were vendors at ballparks and on boardwalks crying out: "Hot dogs! Get your red hots! Buy a pen, get a dog!" (prophetic words).

‍‍‍
ᔆᔆ

Back at the pen plant, the tennis game would have to wait.

In short order, we had almost a hundred employees. And Mom and Zelta were glad to be furloughed. They'd grown tired of the gossip and monotonous work, even though they were as thrilled as we were. But no matter how hard any of us worked or how long the day, our output was still not enough to keep up with the orders.

For a while there, Milt was enjoying the recruitment side of staffing the plant. One morning he showed up with a pair of gorgeous identical twins, Marta and Magda, one on each arm. They were platinum blondes with lots of red lipstick and matching pastel angora sweaters that showed off their round, ample breasts. Fitting them for coveralls seemed a damned shame, but somehow Orville managed it. Milt was pleased with the result and told them they'd soon be posing for ad photos on the factory floor.

We were just beginning to see a whole new side of Milt. Or, at least, a side he'd never let show. The twins were "pen testers." This idea was the first in a long succession of marketing gimmicks. Marketing was supposed to be my department, or one of mine, but then that was back when we had no budget for it.

12

Milt had a private office built on a platform above the factory floor, and glassed in so he could monitor the activity. But he also had it double-glazed so it was almost soundproof.

I walked in on him one morning in mid-November. There was hardly room to move around, there were so many mail sacks. Jesse, our new mail clerk, was just hauling in another one.

"More orders?" I asked.

"That was the morning mail," he answered, indicating the sacks stacked on one side of the room. "These are the telegrams."

"Don't get a hernia, Jesse," Milt called out from behind his desk. "We need all hands on deck."

Good-natured Jesse just smiled. "We got enough orders to float a battleship, that's sure."

To Milt I said, not without an edge, "We'll never fill them all. Admiral."

In fact, we had production going at a good clip, but nowhere near fast enough to fill all the orders in time for Christmas. And Milt knew it.

To Jesse, but meant for me, he said, "We can handle anything they throw at us, can't we?"

"Yessir, we can," Jesse affirmed as he set the bag down. Milt flashed him a big smile as the man left, then he turned and scowled at me.

"You talk like that, what's it do to morale? You're no salesman, and maybe you're no supervisor, either."

"I'm enough of an engineer to know our plant capacity isn't enough."

He clutched a wad of yellow telegrams in his fist and waved them at me. "Do you know what these are? Telegrams from Congressmen. They all want priority status. Ha! Now the shoe's on the other foot!"

"Paperwork czars want pens? Goodness, we do have a problem." My humor was lost on him.

"What you're not seeing is the opportunity. You're framed in on the problem. You fail to get the big picture."

"Our best rate is twelve thousand a day," I quoted to him. "The orders are running at more like twenty thousand. A day."

"How many Congressmen are there, a few thousand?"

"A few hundred," I said.

"Okay, counting their friends and relatives?"

"With our rate of production, we could handle it. If we short everyone else."

"But we *don't have to!*" he insisted. "Even though we have the pens, we play up the same shortage excuse we've told everyone else." He pointed to a photo of President Truman he had on the wall behind him. (Milt was never a Democrat, but wartime makes strange bedfellows. And, of course, he craved that presidential commendation, no matter who was in office.)

"The ones we send—as *gifts*, mind you—we inscribe 'I swiped this pen from Harry S. Truman.'" And he looked like a twenty-pound cat who'd swallowed a thirty-pound canary. "They'll never stop talking about it!"

I had to admit, it was a genius idea, even if it might invite all kinds of complications. Disappointing elected officials, while making them covet your product even more, seemed a risky thing to do.

"You're thinking like a pencil-pusher," Milt said, starting to sound more like a coach than a boss. Never mind that it had taken both his slick tongue and my sharp pencil to get us this far. "You're a pen man, now."

"So how do we take the sharp out of Eversharp?"

He was waiting for this, like a vaudeville comic waiting for his setup.

"Numbered. Gift. Certificates."

Hoo boy! Promissory notes? This really took the cake, and I lost my temper before I could stop myself.

"Since when does chest size have anything to do with testing pens? Excuse me, but this big idea sounds a lot like a big lie. Our customers give us hard cash and they get a *piece of paper?*"

My outburst didn't anger him at all. If anything I suppose my thinking it was a bonehead idea convinced him of its rightness. Then he taunted me with one of his torturous leading questions: "Do you know the difference between a salesman's promise and a lie?"

When I couldn't think of an answer, he said, "He *intends* for it to come true."

This floored me. He wasn't joking. This was his credo. This was how he thought, how he operated.

"Even if it's impossible?" I asked.

"Especially if it's impossible," he insisted.

"You're amazing," I said. But I didn't mean it in a nice way.

I couldn't take any more, at least not right then. I headed for the door, but as I reached for the knob I turned back.

"Do you give me credit for having any intelligence at all? What about the time I got you that airline ticket?"

"What ticket?" as if I'd bought him dozens.

"I got you that ticket to Buenos Aires, and you never asked me how I did it."

"Okay, smart boy. What clever trick did you pull?"

"I walked up to the ticket agent, and I bought it."

And I slammed the door on my way out.

13

That night, Zelta cooked me a hot meal—Chicago comfort food, corned beef and cabbage. With a few boiled potatoes thrown in the pot for good measure, it was a cold-climate meal to be burped and savored all the way till morning. (I suspected she had the recipe from one of our Irish neighbors, which in that part of town could be almost anybody.)

Apparently I did not wolf the meal down as greedily as she had hoped. "In the Mood" was playing softly on the radio, and in other circumstances, a satisfying dinner and an early night under the sheets would have been just the thing.

I recounted for her the scene in Milt's office. Or most of it.

"That's it? That's all you said?"

Actually I thought I'd said quite a lot. I mean, for me.

"Where did you get this recipe? It's—"

"Cut the crap" was what she thought of my attempt to change the subject.

"You know how it is with him."

"Yeah, and I know what it's like with *you*. And with *you* and *him*." Then she muttered, "If I don't take a course or something, I'll go nuts."

"I thought we were, you know, going to start a family." *Why did I pick now to bring this up?* I must've really been desperate to find a different topic of conversation.

Zelta did not scare easily. Milt couldn't get under her skin. "If we got a little Jim or Edna or Zelta," she explained patiently, "it wouldn't be so bad. But the thought of a tiny Milton Reynolds in diapers gives me chills."

Glenn Miller's band hit crescendo, and we could hear the announcer on the radio: "And now, ladies and gentlemen, Fred Allen!"

Applause from the radio audience.

"Say, folks," Allen started in. "Heard about this new contraption, the ballpoint pen?"

"Turn that up," I said to her, and she did.

Allen went on, "Writes under water. Not much use for that. Now, a practical pen would sign the tab when you're under about a quart of liquor."

The radio audience roared with laughter.

Hoo boy!

"Son of a gun," I said.

Allen was on a roll. "The pen Reynolds gave me is inscribed, 'I swiped this pen from Harry S. Truman.' I understand our president has to do a lot of writing—thank-you notes to all the dead people who voted for him..."

More laughter.

"...and notes of apology to anybody who's heard little Margaret sing!"

Much bigger laughter.

Let me offer this explanatory note. Truman himself played passable piano, but our president was particularly touchy about his daughter Margaret's musical talent, or lack of it, despite her arduous efforts. Years later, when the poor girl made a serious attempt to give a public concert, *Washington Post* music critic Paul Hume opined that she had not improved over the years. Then, Truman did pen a letter, but not of apology: "Someday I hope to meet you. When that happens you'll need a new nose, a lot of beefsteak for black eyes, and perhaps a supporter below!" History does not record whether he wrote this blistering missive with a ballpoint. For reasons that will become obvious later in my story, I think not.

Zelta switched off the set with a vehemence that showed her irritation.

"Still think he needs your help?"

"He just came up with that this morning. He must've wired Allen. Well, if you're going to do the impossible, you have to do it right away."

She was livid. "Will you stop being so damned impressed? From what I see, he's just this far from being a scoundrel and a thief."

Wondering whether Allen had more to say, I switched the radio back on. But it was playing "Stardust."

I opened my arms wide, our silent signal to begin that old vertical expression of a horizontal desire.

We danced dreamily, long past the song's ending.

"So you, where do you land?" she asked me.

I kissed her for what seemed a very long time, catching up on a debt I had yet to fully repay.

"I guess I'll never know," I admitted. "Unless I jump."

⁊

The next morning, I awoke fully refreshed, resolved to get on with life, on my own terms. Dressed in my best suit with a new shirt and tie and carrying a new briefcase, I deliberately got off the bus several blocks from the plant so I could enjoy the walk through the south side of the Loop, which was home to some of the big department stores. It was just before Thanksgiving, and the store windows as well as the street itself were decorated for the holiday. The sidewalk was jammed with people in overcoats, all in a hurry during this morning rush hour.

And, during my walk, I rehearsed my speech.

I would be quick and to the point, no drama. The pen was undoubtedly a success. We had made over five million dollars in eight weeks—back when that was real money.

Milt could get along without me.

I stood outside his office door and braced myself to go in.

But as I opened the door, my surprise overcame my resolve. The scene was just too bizarre.

There stood Marta and Magda in skimpy attire. They each held a bushel basket full of greenbacks. On cue, they upended the baskets to dump an avalanche of cash on the seated King Milton. Whereupon several photographers clicked away FLASH-FLASH-FLASH!

"Ha! Ha!" he exclaimed. "Okay, everybody out. I want to be alone with my son and all this beautiful money."

As they all filed out, Milton called after them, "And, boys. See I don't get buried on the society page!"

When they were gone, he rushed over to me. "Quick, lock the door and help me pick up the loot."

I hesitated, caught between his directive and my own desire to follow through on my mission to resign.

"Come on," he urged. "Do you know how much cash this is?"

I locked the door, set my briefcase down, and joined him on hands and knees scuttling around the floor, snatching up the scattered bills.

Still on all fours, we met head-to-head in the middle of the room. I stared him in the eye.

"Zelta and I are going to San Francisco. I'm going to look for a job."

He shoved a fistful of bills in my face. "You'd leave this?"

"Okay," I said as I straightened up. "I'll take some with me."

And with some effort, he also got to his feet.

"This was just a stunt," he explained, indicating the cash. "It all goes back to the bank in an armored car."

He started tossing the gathered bills back into one of the baskets.

"You're a big boy. You want to go, *go!* All of this is yours. Every penny. Or will be someday." He looked up at me with a soulful look that said I'd judged him wrongly. "Take what you need. Okay, take what you want. I only did it for you."

I started filling the other basket with the bills I'd collected. "And here I thought we both did it for you," I said.

He stuffed a wad of bills in my breast pocket. "It won't be any fun without you. God bless. You're staying through the holidays, I hope. Your mother's planned a big Christmas."

I couldn't believe it. I was free!

But I should have suspected something, he was giving in so easily.

There came a knock at the door. Before I could open it, a sheriff's deputy barged in with two official-looking documents in hand.

"Reynolds?" he demanded.

"We both are," I said.

To me, "Milton or James?"

"Jim," I said.

He shoved one of the papers into my hand, the other into Milt's.

"And you would be Milton, then. Consider yourselves served."

He started to go, then added, "And fellas? Don't go leaving town." And then he left.

"What's this all about?" I asked him.

He threw his paper onto his desk, as if it was some unwanted circular. "Opening volley of the battle of the ballpoints. That Straus is so predictable."

"Eversharp is *suing* us?"

"Only fair," Milt said.

"But they don't have a case."

"Actually, they had no choice. Under the circumstances."

"Why?"

"It's a countersuit," he explained. "We served them yesterday. A million dollars. Illegal restraint of trade. So they reply with this weak patent infringement crap."

I took a breath. "Let me get this straight. *We* sued *them?* We have even less reason than they do."

"Our lawyer says Eversharp coerced dealers into canceling orders for our product. Who am I to argue the point? I'm not about to leave money on the table." Milt threw his arm around me, which in the old days, like a month ago, I would have appreciated. "First, you're an engineer. Now you're an attorney? Think *publicity!*"

I shook his arm off and stepped up to him, nose to nose. "Did you somehow guess I was walking out?"

"Had a hunch," he shrugged. "Stick around. It's just starting to get fun."

He had me. He had me, and he knew it.

He reached over and deftly plucked the money back out of my pocket.

"We'll need the cash for legal expenses."

℀

That evening, when I did the honey-I'm-home routine, Zelta of course wanted to know right away how it went. She was worried I hadn't called her.

I told her our plans might have to be put off for a bit.

She took it pretty well, considering. She didn't yell at me or anything. She just excused herself and went for a walk. Without her coat.

It was about twenty degrees outside, and she was gone for a good half-hour. But I guess it's not difficult to stay warm when you're jumping up and down in a mad fury.

14

The exchange of legal suit and countersuit between the Reynolds organization and Eversharp was the opening volley in what became known as the "Pen Wars" in the popular press. Predictably, Eversharp allied with Macy's, the arch-competitor of Gimbels.

The Monday-morning run on Gimbels was written up as "the biggest shopping riot in U.S. history," a dubious distinction that was not surpassed in my lifetime. Of course, Straus followed through on his threat to pull all of his products, but Mr. Fred didn't have a care because the Reynolds Pen continued to outsell any single product he'd ever offered. We had beaten Straus's planned release date by several weeks, and Eversharp hurried to move all of its launch activities up—especially the advertising campaign.

We had no doubt they could ramp up their manufacturing capacity to meet any demand before Christmas. But the real question was whether they could capture the public's imagination in time to outpace our considerable head start in the marketplace.

So Straus pulled out all the stops, dropping more promotion money in the first week than he had originally budgeted for his entire pre-Christmas campaign. He staged his debut event in a high-visibility venue—the line where children queued up to see Santa at Macy's. Except the big event now had nothing to do with kids and everything to do with getting sensational press. And contrary to the original Straus strategy of appealing to the practical lady of the house, he targeted the amped-up publicity event squarely at the ultimate customer—the status-seeking male business executive. Perched prettily on Santa's lap was not some freckle-faced kid pleading for new sled, but a leggy movie star I'd have married in a heartbeat if Zelta hadn't said yes—the sultry, comely Ann Sheridan.

In front of the assembled press corps and a battery of two-dozen Graflex cameras, a beaming, flush-faced Santa handed the eager Miss Sheridan a gleaming Eversharp, held erect in his velvet glove. She took it delicately and bestowed on its tip an exaggerated-pucker, lipsticky kiss.

The flashbulb barrage fired POP-POP-POP, as did the hearts of countless daddies who had suddenly shown an interest in their tots' want lists, and as the lecherous Straus, standing just out of the shot, chuckled with satisfaction, sure now he was right to ignore his wife's advice.

The Reynolds Pen might write under water, but owning an Eversharp could get you laid.

In the coming months and in all propriety, Eversharp would dub its pen model the "CA" for "capillary action." Apparently they hoped anyone who cared, over the long run, would appreciate their Biro-patented design over our gravity-feed workaround.

And also as a counterstroke, Eversharp had intended to undercut us and bring out its pen for ten dollars. But apparently Straus didn't like to leave money on the table either, and in the absence of other competition, he decided instead to raise his price to fifteen.

However, Milt was not to be underestimated, and he had more than a few tricks up his sleeve to keep us ahead of the curve. I wouldn't have thought there'd be time, but he actually launched a second product—the Reynolds Rocket—and *cut* his price. Our ads called it "the atomic-age pen." The name may have been futuristic, but the tone of the campaign was fundamentally caveman—Marta and

Magda posed on either side of a rocket replica as they caressed its tip. Their startled expressions told us this man's machine was ready for blast-off.

Out of nowhere, it seemed, our new product had a theme song. Not only was its title suggestive—"I've Got a Rocket in My Pocket"—but also its suggestive title exceeded Ann Sheridan's mouth job for tackiness.

ೲ

The contest of the Pen Wars also had its spies and its counterspies.

Milt hired a New York publicity flack. Perhaps looking forward to launching in Europe, he chose a flashy Continental type, a Frenchman named André Gaston.

I met this simpering little fellow when we were summoned in haste via telegram from Fred Gimbel. Sheriff or no sheriff, we hopped the next plane to New York.

Fred was probably worried about the lawsuits. But as we ascended to his office in the company of Gaston, whom I'd just met, I wondered what about this dandified pimp was so essential to our getting more media attention.

Dottie's warning look as we entered Fred's office should have been the tip-off.

Milt shoved the guy forward as he made the introduction, "André Gaston, our new *international* PR man."

Gaston grinned and cooed "Enchanté," as he reached in vain to shake Gimbel's hand.

Gimbel rebuffed him with, "Would you excuse us for a moment?" and quickly showed him the door, reclosed it carefully, waited a moment for the fellow to get out of earshot, then turned to Milt.

In a dramatic hush, he exclaimed, "Milton, I know that man! I'm certain he works for Martin Straus!"

Milt was unfazed. "We know he's a traitor. But Straus doesn't."

So in that moment, I made the connection. Straus had a history with the guy, and Milt had hired him away. And the terms of the deal were no doubt that Gaston would continue to also work for Straus, and report back. The risk was he'd also be reporting on us, but knowing Milt he'd have a poison-pill clause in there somewhere so the fellow wouldn't dare.

Gimbel probably assumed as much, too, but it didn't ease his concern. "Reynolds, this time you've gone too far. We went with you. All the way. Straus pulls his merchandise, fine. That frog is Eversharp's man. Now Straus is Macy's man. You've let the wolf into the henhouse, and just in time for Christmas dinner." Then, he turned to me with an earnest expression, a look that said he regarded me as a fellow man of honor. I was immensely flattered. "Jim, did you know about this?"

Milt wanted to keep control of the conversation, of course, and no doubt he had a story all cooked up. But on impulse I realized here was a chance to set myself apart. I didn't plan to stay long in the organization anyway, and with any luck this lawsuit nonsense would be over before it started. So, I guess I figured I didn't have anything to lose, and having Milt in my debt would be capital I could spend someday, maybe soon.

"It was my idea, actually," I lied, "to put one over on Straus. Sorry, Fred. Dad warned me it was a lousy idea."

Gimbel seemed disappointed, but Milt was clearly pleased, and a little surprised, that I'd willingly take the fall for him.

"You will fire this Gaston fellow immediately," Gimbel said. "Now that Eversharp is in, Parker and Waterman won't be far behind. It will take more than cheap tricks to win the day."

Milt offered, "We appreciate your business, Fred." But the meeting was already over.

In the outer office with Dottie, two security guards, apparently summoned by her, already had Gaston in hand.

Milt marched up to him. "Get packing, Gaston! Imagine. A spy for Macy! Have you no shame?"

He didn't answer. All he was prepared to give was name, rank, and serial number. The guards escorted him away, and the Franco-American alliance was one relationship the poorer.

Out in the hallway as Milt and I waited for the elevator, it seemed ironic how much history had been written in the few weeks since we'd last stood here. The ballpoint pen was a national craze, and Milton Reynolds had earned back far more than the last fortune he'd lost.

Milt looked around to make sure Gimbel was nowhere in view, then he gave me a big bear-hug. "Son, I'm proud. It took a lot of guts to take the rap like that."

"So now you're proud of me? For lying to a customer?"

If my sarcasm bothered him, he didn't let it show. "You called me Dad. I'm touched. I really am."

We didn't communicate too well after that, for a long while.

When the time came, Zelta and I dropped around to the folks for a cup of Christmas cheer. For us as a family, the actual holiday was almost a non-event. We'd been working so hard, and the pen had been so successful, by the time the celebration came our emotions were spent. Nothing any of the pen makers threw at the market even began to approach the enthusiasm for the two Reynolds pen models. In fact, we suspected any man opening his gift and finding an Eversharp would, in his heart of hearts, experience a pang of disappointment.

But at Milt and Edna's, with just the four of us (attended by Henrietta), the cocktail talk before dinner had been polite and sparse.

No sooner had we sat down at the table than Mom said, "Jim, there's a turkey I'd like you to meet."

It was a privilege to carve, a man-of-the-house kind of thing, and I was glad she was letting me do the honors.

In the kitchen, Henrietta was at the stove dressing the bird. The arrangement was, she would head home soon to be with her family.

"Henrietta, would you serve the canapés now?" That was Mom's way of telling her she'd stayed long enough.

"I've got to do this turkey," she said. I wasn't sure how happy things were these days at her place, but I was sure she knew she was welcome to eat with us if she preferred to stay. I wasn't particularly proud, though, of the way we were getting along, or not getting along, so I was relieved she decided to go.

"Run along," Mom encouraged her. "Jim is going to do that." And then she asked me, "Care to tell me what's going on?"

"Nothing new," I said.

"You used to at least be able to share a meal with us."

"When do we get to live our own lives?" I hadn't wanted it to sound like a complaint. "Every time I get set to go, he invents some crisis and traps me."

"He's doing this for you."

Yeah, right! "He's doing this for the money. And his monstrous ego."

She didn't get angry with me, but she wasn't about to take sides. "It may come as a surprise to you, but money means nothing to your father. Lately he's been saying he wants to buy another airplane. You know what happened with the other one—the crash, and all."

"It *crashed?*"

"No, no. The stock market. It crashed. He had to sell the thing. I was so glad."

Presumably traveling on business and spreading goodwill, she and Milt had been piloted in the *Flying Printasign* to most of the major cities in South America as they called on prominent retailers. Milt had written long letters back to his friends from each destination—thirty-four letters in all, which the company publicity department eventually collected into a book of memoirs entitled *Hasta La Vista (I'll Be Seeing You)*. They gave boxes of books away to customers. So Milt, the traveling salesman, was now a published book author.

I never knew she hadn't been totally thrilled about going with him. It would probably be news to him, as well.

"The two of you built something." she said, making it sound like a well-coordinated architectural effort instead of what it was, a lucky bet using someone else's idea. "He will lose interest, and it will be yours. And the name will mean something because you, and your integrity, come with it."

"It's not mine," I moped. "It's all his."

"Make it yours," she insisted. "Make it whatever you want. Now go back in there, carve up that turkey, and smile. It's Christmas and you owe me for fourteen months of breast feeding."

It wasn't all smiles and holiday cheer, but we got through dinner without touching on those sensitive topics of when or to where we intended to move, or when we intended to start a family.

ᔕ

The New Year brought new hope. Nineteen forty-six would be the first calendar year in a very long while that some village somewhere in the world wouldn't be invaded or bombed. Probably, it didn't turn out that way. In some remote Pacific islands, they say a few Japanese soldiers kept on fighting.

And the Pen Wars raged on.

At one point during the first year, we had back orders for almost a million pens. The infusion of cash from the Christmas success financed expansion to actually meet demand, which continued to swell. We now employed three hundred workers, and our output increased to about thirty thousand units a day. The phone company brought in fifty phone lines and a switchboard, but sometimes buyers still had trouble getting through. Some reps from distant retail chains showed up in person and had their cabs waiting at the curb to rush them back to the airport. One of them insisted on bumping priority by paying us full retail price for as many as we'd sell him, then went home to offer them without any markup at all. Such was the power of the Reynolds product to lure pen-crazy shoppers into any store.

I was still waiting for the court order to be quashed so I could resign and leave town legally. And so I was reporting regularly to the office.

One morning as I walked from the bus stop, I looked up to see a wrecking ball swing high to take out the side of an old building. New construction was a good sign. Somebody was building something worth keeping.

But it should have been a sign.

The force of gravity can work for you, or it can work against you. But it always works.

The reliable force that caused ink to flow from Reynolds pens was also beginning to take its toll on them. At the office, field reports from the return departments at the stores indicated that some of our worst fears were being realized.

I could just imagine.

At Acme Widgets, an old, sour-faced executive sits behind his desk. He's about to make a bold stroke with his gleaming pen on an immaculate and important document titled, "Last Will and Testament." He looks annoyed as the little blue trail from his pen stops just as he begins to sign. He tries scrawling ever-larger circles in his increasing frustration, hoping the ink flow will resume. He unscrews his pen and squints at the barrel.

Sometimes, you see, a little air bubble would form, and the ink wouldn't flow. Gravity was biding its time.

The man shakes the barrel furiously like a thermometer.

And then sometimes, the little ball fell out.

The ball bearing falls PLINK! from the tip of the pen, followed by a drool of ink, forming a puddle on the hallowed document and running off the desk and into the man's lap as he looks on, dumbstruck.

And even the high and mighty are bound, one day, to fall.

His face turning beet-red, the man crushes the crippled pen in his ink-smeared hand, looks down at the will, then at his ink-stained trousers, and does a slow burn so intense you think he'll catch fire.

Then he gasps and expires, collapsing on his un-signed will.

Okay, perhaps that scenario is a bit extreme. I don't know for a fact that the consequences were necessarily life-and-death.

Consider Maxim's Restaurant in Chicago, one of the toniest places in town. A society couple sits at the best table. They look and act as though they expect the best, probably have servants of their own who either learn how to read their minds or get fired.

Behind a partition, a fearful busboy assists a pompous headwaiter as he dons an immaculate white dinner jacket, checks his grooming, and gets dusted off with a little brush.

The final touch is his gleaming pen, which he tucks proudly into his breast pocket. Then he strides confidently over to the couple's table.

He greets them warmly. Gesturing with his order pad, he begins to recite the long menu to the couple, who seem approving, if not impressed.

The timing of these unfortunate accidents was almost always embarrassing.

As the waiter continues to talk, totally caught up in his recitation, a small blue dot appears along the bottom seam of his coat pocket. To the horror of the onlooking couple, the dot grows and grows, until it is as big as a pie plate.

The waiter talks on, doesn't seem to notice.

Finally reaching for his pen, the fellow looks down to see the stain. Shocked, he clutches his chest, as if he's been mortally stabbed.

Another victim of the Pen Wars, his blue blood gushes from his chest. Furious to the point of insanity, the waiter grabs what's left of his own hair and tries to pull it out, jumping up and down in impotent fury.

Okay, it could've happened that way.

Or then there was the episode at the radio station, maybe at several radio stations. I didn't hear any of those broadcasts, but I do know people were warned.

The banks worried about the law of gravity and rubber checks.

Standing before a cluster of microphones, a fussy matron wearing a pince-nez reads from a script: "The First National Bank of Iowa City has issued the following warning regarding checks written with the new ballpoint pens. Tests have shown the ink will fade, assisting the criminal element in perpetuating forgeries."

Uh-oh. Who knew you could use a pen to fly a kite?

"The only assurance against this calamity," the matron concludes, "is a reliable fountain pen."

I wondered what the likes of Parker or Waterman had to do with this.

ભ

Consumers' Research tested the pens and, sure enough, they concluded the ink was prone to fading. In their review, they also implied that certain disreputable people who didn't want their promises to endure could well exploit this feature.

Bad publicity and worse word-of-mouth caught up with Straus. A bunch of reporters ambushed him on his way into the courthouse.

"No Eversharp ballpoint pen has ever caused any damage to anybody anywhere," he stated flatly. "It's that Reynolds gang."

The way he said it, you'd think it was some lethal drug and we were the pushers.

One of the sharper tacks challenged him, "But you said they stole your design."

"They most certainly did!" Straus shot back, before he realized he'd stepped in it. Then he hastened to add, "But they screwed it up."

Milt and I weren't far behind, on our way to the same appearance. Eyeing the cluster of newshounds, I said to him, "We've got to make good on this somehow. Our name's on every one of those pens."

"Bah," he said. "This is all Eversharp's doing. Propaganda. War is hell."

Was he in denial that our pens were leaking all over the place? Or just glossing over the problem, as he so often did?

However, our brief conversation must have had an impact on him. When a reporter asked him, "Is it only Reynolds pens that leak?" he didn't deny it. (Truth was, all pens leaked, whether fountain-nib or ballpoint and whether capillary-action or gravity-fed. But Reynolds pens leaked more than most.)

To Milt, these distinctions were immaterial. But instead of denying the leakage claims to this reporter, he took the visionary high ground. "With every technological step there are always some—"

And the guy cut him off, "So it's true!"

Then he did something that was every bit as surprising as my taking the rap in front of Gimbel. Maybe he didn't want to be one-upped in the race of the sacrificial lambs. Or his ego was wounded. "I'll personally pay the tab," he said, "to clean any garment soiled by one of our pens."

Okay, he either thought they weren't leaking or that the reports of pens gone bad were greatly exaggerated.

But he should not have said it.

The court appearance was a nonstarter, consisting of preliminary throat-clearing by our attorneys at their sky-high hourly rates.

The next day at the plant, Jesse stuck his head into Milt's office to announce, "People are coming by, dropping off clothes. I don't think they're exactly Goodwill donations. Where do you want 'em?"

Milt was preoccupied, staring through the glass at activity down on the factory floor. "I've got to see this," he said without turning around. "Put them on my desk."

Jesse started to object, but I drew him aside and made a suggestion. I was never one for school pranks, but I felt we had to make a point.

After Jesse left, Milt sat back down at his desk and mumbled, "Straus. Slick Madison Avenue huckster. Reynolds gang! The nerve! I'll show him who's—"

There was a knock at the door, and in came Marta and Magda carrying huge canvas sacks.

They'd obviously gotten into the spirit of the thing, because they started to giggle. And Milt must have thought it was a reprise of the money-dumping gag, because he welcomed them with open arms.

At his desk, they upended the sacks and buried him in an avalanche of stained clothes.

Then they ran out, still giggling.

Milt was furious.

"Quote, put them on my desk. Unquote," I said quietly.

He was already digging through the garments, perhaps assuming he'd have to look hard for tiny smudges.

He held up a white waiter's jacket. It had a bright-blue stain about a foot in diameter on the pocket.

The next day, we received so much damaged clothing we had to get a truck to haul it. I found a dry cleaning establishment to work with us. We got a volume discount, and we stuck with those guys when they came up with a unique solvent for our Satinflo ink, which resisted conventional methods.

But in some cases, no repair was possible, and Milt took drastic measures.

Once again, I could imagine the scene at Maxim's.

The busboy brings the parcel wrapped in brown paper to the off-duty headwaiter. The guy opens the package and lifts out the jacket. There's a big, jagged hole cut out where the stain had been. Appalled, the fellow sticks his hand through it.

The busboy unpins two slips of paper from the garment. He reads, "I have removed the stain. Milton Reynolds." The angry headwaiter grabs the other, neatly folded paper to find Milt's check.

He wrote those checks himself, on his personal account, so I don't know for how much. But he valued his pride. I suspected he was generous and the amount was several times the price of a pen.

And, of course, word of our occasional generous reimbursements just brought us more dry-cleaning business.

Worse for the sake of future business, angry customers were returning pens to Gimbels and demanding their money back.

Summoned once again to Mr. Fred's office and flaunting the advice of our attorneys to stay put, we soon saw the defective products firsthand. Gimbel took us down to a storeroom and showed us bins full of ink-smeared pens.

"The Christmas returns, gentlemen. Thousands of them."

Once again, Milt had a ready reply. "Fred, Fred. Is the glass half empty or half full? You know what I see? Repeat business!"

He had a point. If you thought like a retailer, people coming back into your store for any reason would be an opportunity. Exchange a pen, buy a new dress? How about a discount, something for your trouble?

But Gimbel worried, "What about the leaks? The fading?"

"Fountain pens leak," Milt said with a wave of the hand. "Inkwells tip over."

Gimbel was more eager than I expected to pick up on the repeat-sale idea. "You know," he said, "people wondered about the pen that got the banks so upset. Our sales did pick up for a while, in all departments. And Eversharp wants back in. We expected they wouldn't stay away much past the holiday."

Always ready with his next product demonstration, Milt pulled a new Reynolds Rocket from his pocket. Even though he'd hyped the thing aggressively in the run-up to Christmas, we weren't yet in full production and we weren't shipping that many units yet. Gimbel had been doing so well with the original pen he hadn't paid any attention to the new one.

Milt gestured for him to keep it. "Is this one any better?" he asked, as if studying it would give him a clue.

That's when I chimed in. I didn't want Milt making any more grandiose promises. "You could say it has the benefit of our experience," I said, with a look to Milt that warned him against offering more.

And we didn't waste any time leaving the store.

Outside on Thirty-second Street, the gray January day was blustery and cold. The forecast had a weather front moving in, and we hoped we'd be able to take off before our flight got grounded.

"Nice save back there," Milt said as he waved for a taxi. "We're starting to work like a team. Fred trusts you."

"Are you pulling any punches? Is the new model really better?" I hadn't spent any time with Orville recently, and I naively thought there could have been a design change.

"Well, maybe it would have been if we'd gotten the new ball bearings in time."

I might have known. "Fred won't trust me much longer," I said, "unless we deliver."

Milt pulled his coat collar up against the cold and changed the subject. "Brrr. Kind of makes you think about flying down to Rio."

The cab pulled up, and the topic of conversation shifted as he had the driver get on the radio and ask the dispatcher about conditions at LaGuardia.

On the way to the airport, I thought back to his remark about Rio. He'd said much the same thing that day we came out of Goldblatt's, and then he'd taken off to Buenos Aires. And then there was Mother's mention at Christmas dinner that he was thinking about buying another plane. He wasn't one for making stray comments.

Yes, at one point we'd had a million pens on backorder. But during that same period of time, for multiple valid reasons having to do with failed marketing claims, we'd had to take back more than a hundred thousand of them.

If the ballpoint was to be more than a passing fad and eventually surpass the fountain pen, manufacturers like Eversharp and Parker wouldn't be able to tolerate those numbers. But I also figured they knew how to make better pens. Ken Parker, who had yet to introduce his own model but whose company would end up dominating the market for years, gloated in his newsletter that ours was "the only pen that will make eight carbons and no original." Milton was laughing all the way to the bank, but to me it was not at all funny.

The reality was, by the time we managed to fix all the bugs, we should have sold out.

I knew then, one way or another, Milt was already thinking about getting out of the pen business.

16

We touched down in Chicago in the late afternoon, and the weather was no better. It was colder and with stronger winds, but at least no impending blizzard. The wind, which locals in the Windy City call "the Hawk," blows strongest on Lake Michigan, and our apartment was only four blocks from the lakeshore. But when I got home, I told Zelta to bundle up because I was taking her out to dinner.

There was a Czech place just a block from our house that served Eastern European home cooking, with plenty of starch and gravy, just the thing for warming you against the winter weather. The prices were pretty good, and no matter how overstuffed you got, you had to save room for pastries with homemade chocolate sauce. I knew she couldn't resist it, and I figured I needed help to sweeten things up at home.

By the time we'd gotten through four courses and a layer of apple crumble with ice cream *and* sauce, we were so drowsy it seemed an effort to stumble home. Right then, I supposed my forward planning was shortsighted, in that making love on such full stomachs would be downright uncomfortable. Not that I wasn't willing to try.

Her cheeks were flushed and rosy in the cold. As we paused on the corner to wait for the light to change, I helped her do up her coat. We'd avoided talk of business until then, but the day's events were still on my mind.

I told her about the bins full of sticky pens. "Gimbel was about to take Milt's head off," I said, as if setting up a joke, "and Milt turns it around, convinces him that defective pens bring people back into the store."

She didn't seem annoyed, but right away I knew I'd overstepped.

All she said was "The longer we stay, the more you'll be like him."

"We should stick it out," I said. "Make the company into something that will last."

"Now you sound like Edna." And I realized Mom must have given much the same lecture to her about sticking with it, making the name stand for something.

"God bless the child that's got its own," I said. We were both fans of Billie Holiday.

Then she did something so subtle, so dear, so astonishing. She patted her tummy, looked up at me, and said, "Promise you'll love her just as much if she's a girl?"

I couldn't believe my sly girl had waited to slip me the news in such a fiendishly clever way. When was she planning to tell me? Just as I was falling asleep? In the middle of the night on a bathroom trip?

"You are so beautiful" was all I could say as I kissed her.

"I guess," she said softly as we came up for air, "a steady income doesn't seem like such a bad thing until we're all on our feet."

∽

It's amazing how things fall into place. As I walked briskly to the plant the next morning, I hadn't been so elated since that day at the urinal.

I decided I'd go straight up to Milt's office, barge in, and deliver the news, no matter what he was doing. It would be a fresh start on a new day. It would change everything. We'd both be working toward a new goal, and the Reynolds International Pen Company would be reborn along with our daughter, as a rejuvenated family business.

But the scene in his office was so unexpected, I had to shut up. He was seated as usual behind his desk, but standing over him was the sheriff's deputy who had served us the papers.

But he was dressed in civvies.

Milt was holding a model of a twin-engine aircraft and making buzzing noises with his lips as he waved it around.

Spread out on the table in front of them was a set of blueprints.

"Hey, Jim-boy!" Milt exclaimed.

"Sorry to interrupt," I said. "Sheriff."

The deputy looked up in surprise, turned to Milt, and let out a sniggering chuckle, sounding like a the kid at camp who'd just short-sheeted your bed.

"You guys," he teased Milt. "Always ribbing each other. You never told him?"

Milt looked annoyed, caught in another fib. He set the plane down.

"Jim, meet Bill Odom."

Grinning like a Kansas country boy, Odom stepped toward me to extend a no-hard-feelings handshake.

"Your dad," he grinned. "What a kidder."

I refused to shake. "You're not from the sheriff's department?"

"Don't you read the papers?" Milt chuckled. "This guy is the most famous pilot in the world. Burma, flying the Hump into China?" He indicated the model plane. "We got a chance to buy an A-twenty-six Invader bomber!"

Odom was just as excited. "Strip off her armor, retrofit with a couple of new Pratt and Whitneys, and she'll go like a bat outta hell. Milt wants to go for Howard Hughes's record."

"Around the world in ninety-one hours, fourteen minutes," Milt explained. "You want to go?" As if he were taking a cab ride.

"So those subpoenas were some kind of joke?"

Milt finally came over to me. He could see I was hurt. "Yes and no. Bill's a good sport." Once again, as he'd done so many times before when he wanted to play the father-son card, he threw his arm around me. "You'll come back a hero. The President might even shake your hand. He damn well better shake mine. Think about it."

I shook his arm off. "And the part about not leaving town?"

Milt chuckled again. Those guys really did enjoy their prank. "I thought you'd catch on when we went to see Gimbel. *Twice!*"

"And the money for this new toy?"

Milt was half serious. "You didn't want to stay in the pen business forever, did you?"

"You know I didn't."

Then, too late for the sake of my pride, he said, "You rushed in here like you had something to say."

"It'll keep" was all I said, and I left.

೧

I went straight home, even though it was mid-morning. Zelta was in the kitchen and heard me come in, but I went straight to the bedroom closet for my suitcase. She followed me in, and perhaps at first she thought I'd broken the news and Milt was sending me on some kind of family errand.

"What did he say? Was he happy when you told him? You phoned Edna, didn't you?"

"I have to go to New York," I said as I threw a couple of fresh shirts into my bag.

Zelta was flabbergasted. "Who lives there, *God?*"

"I didn't manage to tell anybody anything."

"Never tell him about the baby? Well, there's an idea. Sure that won't, I don't know, just offend him more?" She realized applying logic wasn't going to explain anything I'd decided to do because of Milt. "What does he want you to do now?"

"I've been an idiot," I said. I didn't want to tell her my whole plan, both because it wasn't fully formed and because, if I did, I was afraid she'd talk me out of it. "I need a new job."

Early the next morning, in the wee hours just before dawn, my DC-3 banked over the Manhattan skyline on my second approach to LaGuardia in as many days. By now the storm had passed through and the sky was crystal clear. The city lights looked like jewels nestled in black velvet. It was a magical place where fortunes were made and lost every day.

I was finally doing something for myself. So why did I feel like such a creep?

ↄ৴

The corner of Martin Straus's office was done up like the smoking room of a gentlemen's club. He had bookcases lined with leather-covered books and posh, overstuffed armchairs. And I held one of his premium cigars, which I'd puffed just long enough for him to light it for me. I was hoping we could get to the point quickly so I didn't have to smoke it all the way down.

"I want to work for you," I said.

He smiled. "More than you do already?"

I could tell I would not enjoy his brand of humor very long.

"How's that?"

"Every time Milt gets in the papers, we sell a boatload. Pen business has been good to everybody. Joke is, you guys never did anything wrong."

What was I hearing? "You *know* we didn't infringe on the patent?"

Then Straus made what I thought was a stunning admission. Other pen manufacturers, both small and large, were coming out with models that copied the Biro capillary-action design. They were emboldened by the mistaken assumption that the Reynolds organization had gotten away with it. But, in truth, we were alone among them in not having done anything wrong. Gravity was indeed in the public domain, as was John Loud's roller-bearing scheme.

But Straus wasn't about to lift a finger to sue those infringers. Why? Because he realized, to his profound chagrin, he'd be doing Milt's work for him by eliminating our competition—in effect, handing us a monopoly.

"It's a game, Jim," he said coolly, crossing his legs. "Milt can tell you. Competition's good for business." He took a long, satisfying drag. "But now there are too many players. You can't beat the big boys forever. My advice to Milt was to sell out, and soon."

Milt was way ahead of me! And maybe I had yet to realize how far.

"Nothing like a good Havana," Straus cooed. "Bad form, I suppose, offering you your father's cigars."

All through the legal battles, all through the name calling and the "exclusive" negotiations with Fred, Milt had been having a backchannel conversation with the devil himself.

I didn't know what to say. "There's the family name to think of." I meant to change the topic to the future of the pen business, to somehow making good on the value of the brand. Looking further out, Eversharp had the added advantage that their capillary-action pens leaked a lot less often than ours did.

"Oh, the Reynolds name will always stand for something," Straus beamed, and I thought he'd say something generous and memorable. "Brass balls!"

༺༻

Back home in Chicago and unable to sleep, I'd kept Zelta awake as I recounted how my plans of betrayal had backfired in my face.

"So Milt set you up again," she observed, stating the obvious but not rubbing it in. "Why am I not surprised?"

"Straus said we'd be smart to sell out now. And he thinks Milt's lost interest."

"Don't count on it," she said and turned on her side and drifted off to sleep.

17

The family got the news of the baby when Zelta broke it to Mother, whereupon they shifted into delighted, high-gear planning mode. I didn't speak of it directly to Milt, who rightly guessed it was what I'd wanted to tell him so urgently the day I found Odom in his office. But he wrongly guessed it meant I would stick with the family business forever. Or, I hoped he was wrong.

One reason we didn't talk about it was he left town soon afterward, caught up in his own manic planning. He'd already ordered the plane, which had been flown up to the Pratt & Whitney plant in Connecticut, where it would be reworked and get a shiny, new pair of the latest, fastest Wasp air-cooled radial-piston engines. In the final weeks of assembly, he went out to supervise, and then Bill Odom was there to go through his checklist.

When the plane was ready, he and Odom took it on its maiden voyage from Hartford back to Meigs Field on the edge of Lake Michigan.

Zelta, Mom, and I took a cab out there to see them touch down.

He'd renamed it the *Reynolds Bombshell*. Painted on the side of the cockpit was a big emblem, continuing in the fine tradition of the Pen Wars—a buxom, scantily-clad babe stroking a pen as big as she is.

Milt and Bill climbed out of the cockpit and down the wing, standard procedure for exiting the plane. Milt looked clownish, I thought, in his flight suit, leather aviator's cap, and goggles. But considering the privilege of wearing that outfit was the cost of the plane, his costume was far from laughable.

And the way he grinned, you'd think he'd stepped out of a dime novel.

We couldn't go too far out on the tarmac because the engines were still running, and we couldn't get caught in the prop wash. The women held back, and I went out to greet the three aviators.

"What do you think?" Milt yelled. "Hear those engines!"

"A dream come true," I yelled back.

He got closer and drew me aside. "Why didn't you tell me you were talking to Straus?"

"Why didn't *you* tell *me?*"

"Why didn't you tell me about the baby?" For that one, I had no good answer.

"Are you selling out?" I asked him.

"Maybe," he said. "But not to you."

As Mom came up and he gave her a kiss, he said to her, "Bill says I'm down to my flying weight." Indeed, he'd lost thirty pounds so he could fit through the aircraft hatch.

"Why don't you fly to Milwaukee a few times, for practice?" she asked.

He gave her another affectionate peck on the cheek.

"Bill doesn't need any practice. And me, I'm just along for the ride. Sure beats working for a living, right Zelta?" I don't know what he meant by that, and I guess she didn't either. Then he embraced her quickly and added, "I'm happy about the kid. Thrilled, even."

So that was the eventful reunion. Of course, the plane was his baby. And all he could think about was flying around the world and knocking Howard Hughes off his perch.

Later that evening, we had dinner at their place. Afterward, in a private conversation, his mood changed.

"I should be the one to apologize," he said. "It took guts, what you did."

I didn't waste words. There was no point. "Zelta and I are going to Los Angeles. There are lots of jobs in aviation. I'll make 'em, you fly 'em."

"Go," he surprised me by saying, and without sarcasm. "With my blessing."

"You mean it? You swear we're finally done with pens?"

He hesitated a moment, as though he knew the size of the favor he wanted greatly exceeded his credit with me. "There is one loose end, needs tying up. Do this thing for me, and you can go. Or you can buy the business for a dollar. Whatever makes you happy."

He really did want to fly around the world. More than anything, apparently.

"Gimbel likes you," he went on. "Pay him one more call."

And he explained to me the offer I would make to Fred, which, like the deal he hinted he'd give me, seemed uncharacteristically generous.

જ

Gimbel suggested we meet at his house. He was working a long weekend away from the phones at the office, he said.

From New York, I took the New Haven Railroad to Darien and his driver met me at the station. From the royal treatment, it seemed I'd moved into his inner circle.

It was mid-March of 1947, and we took advantage of a brief spring thaw to get in a soggy round of golf at his club.

As he teed up, I was telling him my plans. "So, I'll be making them and he'll be flying them. It's the right time to get out. Straus and the others can fight over what's left."

He selected his wood and squared off for his shot. "You boys are cashing in while you're ahead. I can respect that." His club face met the ball SMACK! in an expert drive up the center of the fairway, sailing high and sure toward the pin.

"There's an opportunity here for you, Fred." I explained as I fumbled to get my ball to stand on the tee. I was concentrating on picking my words rather than setting up the shot. "You stuck with us, and we owe you. We've still got a good-sized inventory, say, eighty-thousand pens. You can have them for ten cents on the dollar. Milt's way of saying thank you."

As I stepped up to address the ball, I didn't realize I was holding a putter. I was on my backswing as I delivered my pitch, "Sell them for half price and take the sharp out of Eversharp."

Gimbel reached out to touch my arm, gently took my putter, and exchanged it for his driver.

"Here," he said. "You'll do better with this."

෯

Gimbel gave us the order, and we shipped him the pens. Milt held back a few as giveaway items for his trip. He would have to make a minimum of four refueling stops—in Egypt, India, China, and some island near Alaska. If things didn't go well, Milt might find out whether the Reynolds Pen could write under ice.

I hardly saw him anymore. I couldn't imagine what all he had to do. Outfitting the plane for a week-long tour didn't seem like a month-long chore. They'd have some food and emergency supplies, of course. But they'd take as little as possible to conserve weight, boost their speed, and save fuel. And they'd resupply at the refueling stops.

Since the pen business was winding down and Milton was nowhere in sight, my days at the office were much more relaxed. I'd sent out letters asking about jobs, but it didn't seem as though I'd make much headway until we were out there. We were making our own plans to pick up and move, but we had little more than a few suitcases. We weren't about to go shipping our modest furniture out there.

One evening Zelta and I decided we'd treat ourselves to a movie. As I returned from the lobby with sodas and a big box of buttered popcorn, Zelta grabbed my arm. "I can't believe it. This time next week we'll be toasting our toes in Southern California."

"Sure you don't want to stay for Milt's flight? It should be exciting."

And it wasn't but a minute into the Movietone newsreel that we got a preview of Milt's exploits. There he was in his business suit, standing with Bill Odom, who was in his flight suit. Milt waved a fistful of ballpoints at the camera.

The voiceover narrator told us, "Peripatetic penman Milton Reynolds will be passing out Bombshells—goodwill gifts from Yanks—at refueling stops from Cairo to Karachi to the Island of Canton."

They switched to Milt at the microphone, as he announced, "I named my new pen after my incredible airplane." Indicating the pen, he said, "The new Reynolds Bombshell is guaranteed not to leak, even at twenty thousand feet. I'll be writing up my flight logs with one."

Up came the newsreel music fanfare as Milt shook hands energetically with Odom for benefit of the cameras. They were both all grins and waves, like in some home movie.

As the house lights in the theater went back up before the feature, Zelta could see I was as angry as I'd ever been.

Getting out of the pen business? Oh, really? During the time I thought he was planning his trip, he must have been orchestrating the launch of this brand-new pen model. Did he have just a few prototypes, or was he in full production somewhere else—like Eversharp?

He'd said the new pen wouldn't leak—*guaranteed.* And I was the one who had sold Fred Gimbel eighty thousand of the old model. The ones we all knew *would* leak.

℘

The next day at the office, Gimbel gave me more details on the phone. As bad as the situation seemed, I had not yet appreciated the depth of Milt's betrayal, of both of us.

Having buried the hatchet, or so they thought, Straus paid a courtesy visit to Fred in his office.

"No hard feelings, Martin?" Fred smiled graciously. "We're thrilled to have Eversharp products back in our store." Then he handed him one of the original-model Reynolds pens. "Here, with my compliments. Collector's item. We bought up the rest of Reynolds' stock for pennies."

"How many did you get?"

"Why, eighty thousand! Didn't cost me much more than ten grand."

Straus couldn't contain his amusement as he handed Gimbel a pen from his own pocket. "Try this one. It's called the 'Bombshell.'"

"Your new model?" Obviously, Gimbel did not suspect he'd been duped.

"It's the new Reynolds pen," Straus said. "Two pens in one. Writes in red and blue."

"The bastard," Gimbel grumbled. "Sticking me with all those useless old ones. What did you do, steal one of their prototypes?"

"No," Straus admitted. "I just walked in and plunked down my ninety-eight cents. At *Macy's*. You see, he's screwed *both* of us."

The renewed competition in the Pen Wars had caused prices to plummet. What was a luxury gift a few months ago was now a commonplace office-supply item. And the new price of the Bombshell—less than a buck—was not even a tenth what the original pen sold for, and very close to Gimbel's cost for the junk pens. So he wouldn't be able to undercut the new pen's price without losing money. And even if he did so, consumers would quickly realize it was an inferior product.

As he finished his story on the phone, Fred reminded me, "'Milt's way of saying thank you,' you said."

I didn't have an excuse to offer. I assured him I'd been blindsided as well. But I'm not sure he believed me.

18

Zelta met me at the office after work, something she rarely did. I knew something was up. We sat at the bar at Lulu's in silence for what seemed a very long time. Silent, that is, except for the clinking of ice cubes in my Early Times and then the sound of her sucking the last of her soda with a straw.

"Know what that means in Swahili?" she asked me.

"Nope," I said, hardly looking up from my drink. I'd had so much I could hardly hold my head up.

"Means it's all gone," she said.

It was kind of funny, but I couldn't manage a chuckle. I took another long pull to drain my glass and signaled to Lulu to pour another.

"You stopped being fun an hour ago, or was it last year?" Zelta said, not angrily but not joking, either. As Lulu came back over, Zelta said to her, "Call me a cab?"

Lulu shot me a look but poured anyway. Through my mental fog, I realized my wife was not just going back to our place.

"You packing your bags?" I tried not to sound like the wounded party. I knew I deserved it. She was fed up with me. I was fed up with me.

"I never unpacked," she said and slid off her bar stool.

"Explains why we never bought any good furniture," I said.

She gave me a peck on the cheek. "I guess this is where I say I'm going home to Mother."

She left, and fool that I was, I stayed.

When I wanted Lulu to pour again, she put her hand over my glass. "Your best friend get his legs shot off? Your wife got cancer?"

"How do you tell your own father he's surpassed your lowest expectations? And then how do you deal with the thought you're no better than him?"

"We're talking about Milton? Don't expect anything, for starters. Writes under water. I have yet to figure that one out."

"Just when I thought I was away clean. I thought I had it all worked out. Maximum respect, minimum guilt. Then, whammo. Now, if I go, it looks like I'm running away like a beaten dog."

"Well, if the beaten dog's got someone to cuddle with, maybe it's not so bad," she said, as she capped the bottle and mopped up, her not-so-subtle way of telling me I was cut off. Then she looked me in my bleary eyes and said, "If you're staying, you better stand up to him."

I tried to manage a smile. "Now, why didn't I think of that?"

I was thinking of going, and I was just going to rest my head on the bar for a moment, but I must've fallen asleep.

The next thing I remember was the incredibly comforting feeling of fingers running through my hair. I looked up, thrilled that Zelta had come back for me.

But instead, there was my Mother. I could see both fury and compassion in her face.

ભ

We stood on the el platform waiting for the train. We hadn't said a word to each other since she'd taken me by the arm, helped me off my chair, and led me out of Lulu's. I sipped from a paper cup, black coffee courtesy my barkeep shrink. I didn't actually know where we were headed. We were on the wrong side of the tracks for a northbound train to my place. I supposed we were going to theirs. She'd sit me down in the kitchen, sober me up, and then I'd get the long lecture.

Okay, I deserved it.

"I didn't become what he wanted me to be," I finally said.

"No," she said. "You're everything he wanted for himself, everything he's actually not. And he's jealous."

I figured she was trying to build up my ego. I couldn't imagine Milt could be jealous of anyone.

"If the weather breaks," she went on, "they're flying tomorrow. I'm asking you to stay in town, only until he's back. Three or four days. That long can't matter."

"Mom," I said. "Zelta is leaving me."

"You'll have time to get her back. But your father is leaving, too. And, I don't want to jinx things by saying this, but there's a chance he won't come back."

"Oh, come on!"

"No one will tell me what the risks are, but I have a fair idea." I could see she'd been trying to prepare herself for the worst, probably keeping it to herself for weeks. "If you won't do this because I'm asking you, then please do it because you might never see him again."

She certainly knew how to play on my heartstrings. I didn't for a minute think there was any chance of Milt's not making it. He never seemed to run out of luck, even when it looked like everything would go bust. "Did he put you up to this? Sounds like another one of his tricks."

She wouldn't answer that. As far as she was concerned, I was stuck on my own worries, not really thinking about hers. "He's still at the office. After your head clears, take our car, drive over there, and pick him up. Have your talk. Say whatever you have to say. Zelta and I will take a cab and meet you at the airfield."

She didn't understand. By now, Zelta would probably already be at Midway, ready to board a plane for Denver, where her parents now lived. "Mom, she's not..."

"I admit I was put up to this," she said. "Talking sense into you."

"I thought so."

"But not by Milton. You married the right girl. Never forget that."

Maybe Zelta was having second thoughts? Or was she just humoring Mom through the crisis with Milt? "It looks like rain" was all I said.

༜

While I sobered up and went to pick up Milt, Edna went to get Zelta to go to Meigs. They got there first, for reasons I will soon explain.

For the official record, the globe-circling flight would originate from LaGuardia in New York. I suppose that's because Milt wanted it to end there—to maximize the exposure in the international press. But he'd been tending to business in Chicago right up to the last, and his precious plane was still here, parked on the edge of the tarmac after its test run.

It had been raining on and off all day. I don't know why they wanted to start the flight at this particular time, but it probably had something to do with wanting to eventually touch down in daylight, so the newsworthy event could get good photo coverage.

At the airfield, Odom was briefing copilot Tex Sallee on the flight plan. They'd actually been intending to take off for a couple of days, but first the weather and then their equipment gave them trouble. The last glitch was a defective radio on the A-26, which needed a part that had to be flown in from Hughes on the West Coast.

Mom and Zelta were met by a small cadre of reporters, who were all looking rumpled and listless since they'd already been waiting for hours. Mom had nothing to tell them and so they left her alone and went back to their naps and card games.

Odom walked over to her. "So, where's Milt?"

"He and Jim are coming from the plant," she said. "I thought they might be here by now." She was obviously worried.

"I'm sure they'll be here any minute," Odom said as Sallee joined them. "Ma'am, this is Tex, our flight engineer." In fact, Sallee was both navigator and copilot. Milt was just along for the ride.

The kid smiled at her bashfully. He was younger than me, barely twenty. He must have gotten his wings just as the war ended.

"Does Milt get to fly the plane?" Mom asked.

"We might be brave," Odom replied. "But we're not stupid." I bet Zelta got a kick out of that one.

Turning to the reporters, he announced, "Storm's about blown out. First break in the clouds, we go."

One of them shot back, "You guys wouldn't be trying to milk this story?"

Mom walked right up to the news guy. "Now listen to me. Milton Reynolds is not out to kill himself so you people can have a story. If you don't want to put anything in your paper about it, why don't you all go home right now?"

‸

We were in his big Buick sedan, and I was driving. There had so far been no man-to-man talk, no full and frank exchange of views. I'd told him Mom asked me to give him a lift to the airfield. He'd tidied his desk, and we got in the car. Neither of us had said a word since we left the plant. We were soon traveling outside the city on a rural road, and the rain was coming down in windblown sheets. He was none too happy with the weather, which of course was none of my fault, nor with my driving, which I guessed he thought was not fast enough, despite the obvious need for caution.

"I should have taken a cab," he said.

I knew this was a dig about my driving and not my navigation, but I said, "I know where I'm going."

"Watch the road" was his reply.

I was going fast enough the tires squealed on the wet curves. I had the wipers going full speed, but they couldn't keep up with the downpour, and my visibility wasn't all that good.

All this said, had I been going slower or had the wipers worked better or had the rain been any lighter—I still wouldn't have been able to prevent what happened next.

There was a blinding flash in the sky, a deafening CRACK! and an immense tree toppled. The black, gnarly thing loomed toward us in the middle of the road.

"Watch out!" Milt cried.

My reflexes kicked in, I jerked the steering wheel to swerve—but not so much to send us into a spin. We missed the tree, but one of the tires hit something in the ditch and BLAM! it went flat.

The car lurched to a stop like a crippled giant.

I was just glad we hadn't hit the tree. Or rolled over.

We both gasped as we caught our breath from the adrenalin rush of the close call.

The only sound besides our excited panting was the splatter and din of rain banging down on the car roof. To me, it was a drum roll leading up to my execution. He wouldn't be so much thrilled we'd survived as furious he'd been delayed.

Out here in this remote area, there was nothing to do but get out and change the tire ourselves. We'd soon be soaked, but we had no choice.

"Let's get on with it," he said.

It was a challenge just wrestling the jack and the spare out of the trunk. The rain made everything slippery, and we kept losing our grip.

The heavy spare tire fell out of my hands and onto the ground.

"You get this fixed, and I'll drive," he fumed. "Can you hurry it up? I've got a plane to catch."

Finally I stood up. I left the tire on the ground. "Just when were you going to tell me about Macy's?"

It was ridiculous challenging him while we stood there getting drenched, but I was past being able to control my temper.

"We had to keep Gimbel in the dark until the last minute."

"You might have told me."

"Are you kidding? Gimbel could read your nice-boy face like a ticker tape."

"We lied to him, and you lied to me."

Until now he'd been nasty, but mostly annoyed. Now he turned on me with a fierceness I had not seen in a long time. "It's a tough world out there! Hadn't you noticed? They had to fight a war because nice guys like you let the Nazis go too far."

Oh, now World War II was all my doing? "So now I'm a coward?" He knew I was sensitive about not having served because of my allergies. Neither of my parents had wanted me shipping out, but whenever he wanted to get me riled, he knew rubbing this in would do the trick.

I went back to work putting the jack together and wedging it under the car. This argument wouldn't solve anything.

"You got a lesson in playing dirty," he said, returning to the subject of our screwing our business partners. "We won. Straus and Gimbel lost."

I was able to start jacking up the car. No congratulations from him, of course.

"This stunt with the plane," I said without looking at him. "It's all about your huge, bloated ego, isn't it?" Then I looked up at him. He was shocked I'd call him out. He thought he would be the one delivering the lecture. "You could *die*—to prove what?"

"I won't die!" he yelled as he struggled to roll the spare over to me through the mud. "I promise you!"

"No one can promise that."

I was crouching on the ground. He bent down to my level and said in my ear, "I intend for it to be true."

I got up, pulled back my soaking shirt, and bared my stomach, just like we used to do. Only this time it wasn't a parlor trick. But somehow I figured, if he was going to abuse me, this way would be better, more honest.

"Go ahead. Take your shot," I dared him. "You know you want to."

I could see him hesitate. And for a passing moment I think he really did want the satisfaction of hitting me instead in the jaw and knocking me out cold. But he hauled off and gave it to me squarely in the gut. And he pulled his punch.

Not that it didn't hurt.

I lunged at him and threw my arms around him in a bear hug. I bared my teeth and let out a fearsome "Arrgggggg!" I wanted it to sound threatening, but maybe he thought I wasn't serious.

We toppled over into the muck, where we struggled for several minutes.

❧

Back at the airfield on the lakeshore, the rain had let up. Tex was in the cockpit of the Bombshell cranking up the starboard engine. Odom was on the ground inspecting the fuselage as he checked off items on his clipboard.

We pulled right up onto the runway in the Buick and skidded to a stop. He'd let me drive, after all.

We climbed out and were met by Mom, Zelta, and the contingent of reporters. Milt and I were muddy from head to foot, and some dried blood was caked around his nose.

"Sorry to worry you, dear," he said sheepishly to Mom.

"Goodness! What on Earth happened to you?"

I threw my arm around Milt and explained, "We had to change a tire."

Milt beamed proudly as though I'd won a scholarship or been named salesman of the year. "He gave me a bloody nose!"

Seeing us, all Zelta could say was "Men."

19

Dawn was breaking in a clearing sky as Milt, Odom, and Tex posed in their flight suits on the wing of the Reynolds Bombshell. They hammed it up for the news photographers, and Milton, of course, waved a fistful of the new pens.

You'd think they were three lodge brothers off on a fishing trip.

And after our father-son "talk," I wouldn't say we were fully reconciled, but at least we had an understanding. Each was letting the other go his separate way, and I hoped there was a measure of respect.

Milt was ready to be a kid again. And play with his new toy.

They flew from Meigs to LaGuardia, where they were met by clearing skies and a much larger press corps. And on April 12, 1947, the momentous flight finally commenced.

Their first refueling stop was Gander in Newfoundland. Their tanks were nowhere near empty at that point but had to be topped up for crossing the Atlantic. A crowd of excited villagers met the plane. Milt and the boys posed for pictures with a family bedecked in furs. Milt gave a pen to each of them.

The Atlantic crossing was uneventful. Their flight path arced up over Iceland, but they didn't need to put down. It was much more important, after all, to beat the record than to give away pens.

As they caught sight of the Irish coast, Odom called out, "Damn, this baby is fast! Milt, we got enough fuel, what do you say we skip Shannon?"

Never mind there was a whole press corps waiting for them there, including a couple dozen schoolchildren dressed like leprechauns. But, again, beating the record was the main consideration. It would take just as much time to land, refuel, and take off from Paris as from Shannon. But getting ahead of schedule by a couple of hours could make a difference later, especially if there were unexpected delays.

Tex answered for everyone when he exclaimed, "Yahoo, Paree!"

Perhaps Milt was thinking about getting his picture taken with a gaggle of Parisian lovelies when he wondered out loud, "How tall is Howard Hughes?"

And, indeed, the highlight of the Parisian stopover was a reception committee composed of a chorus line of beauties from the Folies Bergère. Tex was a kid in a candy store as Odom supervised the refueling and Milt gifted them all with pens. The girls' costumes had no pockets, so to the delight of all including the photographers, the girls giggled uncontrollably as they lasciviously stuck the pens in their cleavage.

The unexpected delay didn't come until they landed in Cairo. During the landing at Farouk Field, the plane blew a tire (just when Milt might well have thought he'd satisfied his karma in that department). But Odom's instincts paid off. The time it took to change the tire just about consumed the two-hour lead they'd gotten by avoiding Shannon.

There's a news photo of Milt on the runway at Farouk posing with a camel. He's holding the pen in one hand and pointing to the camel's hump with the other. Aficionados of the ballpoint will get the joke when they remember Milt's ad slogan, "This veritable camel of a pen won't ask for a drink…"

Tire fixed, their next stop was Karachi, in the British colony of Pakistan. As in Egypt, the photo opportunity featured pack animals, this time llamas. Milt gave the nomads pens, but they were unsure of what to use them for.

Even though they still had fuel, they put down in Calcutta for the same reason they'd stopped in Gander. They needed to top off the tanks before crossing the Himalayan mountains.

To this day, don't go to Calcutta (or anywhere in India, really) without plenty of ballpoints to give the kids.

But on takeoff from Calcutta, Odom struggled with the stick, which began to wobble uncontrollably. The expedition was well past the half-way point, and they'd all been in high spirits. Milt got testy when he thought there'd be another delay.

Odom set the plane back down, cut the engines, and taxied to a stop.

I shudder to imagine what it was like, spending four days with Milton in a space the size of a closet.

"Bill, don't tell me we have another flat tire."

"Worse," Odom said, "we lost our hydraulics. It's back to the hangar."

"How long?" Milt wanted to know.

"Long as it takes" was all Odom would say.

Like the best veteran pilots, and especially those who'd flown in wartime, Odom was cool under fire. Milt's sarcasm would be lost on him. But there was at least one incident during the flight when the crusty flyboy probably wanted to throw Milt out of the bomb-bay doors.

They had to fly at their highest altitude—about twenty-thousand feet—to cross the Himalayas. The view of the brilliant, snow-capped peaks was spectacular. They needed their oxygen masks because the air is both cold and thin up there. The risk, of course, is shortness of breath with consequent loss of consciousness if you can't get enough oxygen into your bloodstream fast enough.

And, it turns out, the risk is all that much higher if you are in the company of a traveling salesman.

As they ascended over the mountains, Odom started to choke at the controls. The air in his tank was almost gone.

"Take the stick," he gasped to Sallee, and he pleaded, "Tank! Spare tank!"

Taking over the controls, Tex yelled to Milt, "He's out of oxygen! Put him on the spare tank!"

Milt was confused and didn't know what to do right away. But Tex couldn't help, because it was all he could do to fly the plane.

Meanwhile, Odom passed out, slumping into his seat.

"Will you get a move on?"

Milt had trouble getting out of his harness. The heavy gloves they were wearing against the cold prevented him from working the buckles. He finally wriggled out and crouched down to look under Odom's seat for the pilot's reserve tank. Where it should have been, there was no tank, just a plain cardboard box.

"I forgot," Milt said to Tex. "I stowed it aft."

"Give him yours!"

Milt was really panicked now, especially at the prospect of having to give up his own air.

"Do it!" the copilot screamed.

Milt ripped off his gloves and reached over to pull Odom's mask aside. Then he took off his own and shoved it onto the pilot's face. Milt held his breath until his face turned red as Odom coughed, took a gulp of air and then another. As the pilot started to come around, Milt got the idea of buddy breathing, like scuba divers do, and they alternated using the mask for a while.

"Where's the reserve tank?" Odom asked him after his head cleared and he was out of danger.

Milt smiled weakly. "I had to make room for the pens."

Dropping out of the clouds from the mountain elevation, the plane's next stop was Shanghai. The Chinese people loved their pens, but of course the grim-faced Red soldiers wouldn't let them write anything!

Then, in Yakota, Japan, Milt presented a pen to a U.S. Army officer, a member of Gen. MacArthur's occupation force, who accepted it on behalf of the Japanese people. (Despite this precaution, they eventually copied it anyway, and the Japanese version didn't leak.)

As they did over the Atlantic, the plan for crossing the Pacific called for staying within sight of land wherever possible. That mean flying up to Vladivostok on the edge of Russian Siberia, and from there arcing around the Bering Strait and into Alaskan airspace.

But plans changed when it turned out the Russians weren't expecting company.

"Russkies just took in the welcome mat," Odom reported as he signed off the radio. "Looks like we go the long way around."

The Russians may have been suspicious the Bombshell was doubling as an American spy plane. It wasn't a particularly far-fetched idea in those days. Or maybe they were fresh out of black pepper to put in the guests' vodka. But in any event, waving the plane off meant not only that the boys couldn't land, but also they'd have to skirt Russian airspace, flying farther out to sea than they'd planned.

Milt had been keeping notes faithfully in his flight log. He was doubly pleased with himself as he recalled that writing at altitude was the original use of the Myles Aircraft version of Biro's pen.

Consulting his log, he said, "We're four hours ahead of the record. Will this cost us time?"

"Maybe only an hour or two at full throttle," Odom calculated.

Tex asked him, "Bill, we got enough fuel for that?" Increasing speed to make up time and distance had a cost in fuel. Even Milton knew the risk. If they had any problems out over the sea, they'd have to ditch the plane in the water.

All Odom wanted to know was "How close do you want to cut it, Milt?"

Milt thought a moment and then said, macho as any pilot, "Hell, I can swim."

Odom grinned at Tex. They wanted to go for it, too. Never mind that if they landed in the Arctic water, it really wouldn't make a difference whether you could swim.

20

About the time the boys were hoping they wouldn't be forced to drop in on the polar bears, I was trying to not to think about Milt or the future of my career by working feverishly alongside Zelta to paint the baby's room.

Deciding this room would be the baby's and then deciding to paint it took the place of having a discussion about staying in Chicago. How long that decision would be in force was an open question.

I was trying to get my brushstroke to follow a straight line but not having much success. "I was never any good at this," I huffed. Then I turned to her and gestured toward the new crib. "So now we're buying furniture?"

"Babies have a way of showing up wherever you happen to be at the time," she said. "Besides, she will appreciate we brought her back to a nice, cheery room." She took my brush, dipped it in the paint, and handed it back. "It's like Edna's knitting. Keeps your mind off other things."

"I said a lot of things to him I shouldn't have."

She wasn't about to share the sentiment. "He *did* a lot of things he shouldn't have."

"Sometimes I hated him. Maybe most of the time. More than once, I actually wished he was dead. But now if anything happens…"

"Shut up and paint," she said.

༄

They were at least a half-hour from the westernmost of the Aleutian Islands when they hit severe weather. They were flying through an icy thunderstorm, with a gale-force headwind. Odom had tried to find a clearing by changing altitude, but so far no luck with that.

The buffeted plane shook wildly and every now and then bucked in a gust. Flashes of lightning made the cockpit briefly light as day.

"This headwind is a bitch," Odom cursed. "What've you got on fuel?"

Tex had Milt's clipboard and tried to hold it still long enough to check the fuel-consumption, airspeed, and distance calculations.

"We're sucking it up like a sailor on a binge," he pronounced. Then he caught himself. "Whoa. Sorry guys, looks like I figured wrong."

The other two just stared at him.

"We can't make it to Anchorage at this rate," Sallee admitted.

Odom was pissed. He couldn't do much about running out of fuel, but he could expect a navigator to get the consumption figures right.

"Ever been ice fishing?" was his way of telling them they'd have to ditch.

Milt's eyes grew wide. "We're gonna make it, right?"

ᘒ

We spent that night at Mom's. That way, we'd get out of our house and avoid the paint fumes, we'd be able to offer her our emotional support, and Zelta could go to bed as early as she liked.

It was after dinner. The phone rang. It was the liaison office Milt had set up to handle publicity. It wasn't a long conversation. Her tears came quickly.

"You'll call us back the minute you know?" she asked the caller. "Whatever hour of the day or night, you call me. Okay? Okay."

She came over and wanted a hug.

"It's going to be all right," I said, and I tried to sound a hundred-percent sure.

"They lost radio contact and hour ago," she told us. "They say storms at sea are so violent. And the fuel. They had just enough before all this, and then the weather..."

"Milt's tougher than any old storm," Zelta said, doing her best to make it sound respectful.

"And Bill has been through a lot worse," I added.

"I don't know, I don't know," Mom sobbed, not holding back now. "This time he may have really gone and done it!"

We didn't say much to each other after that. After an hour or so, Zelta had fallen asleep on the couch. Henrietta had stayed and brought me some coffee as Mom curled up next to me in her chair.

"If we lose him..." she finally wailed out loud.

"We're not going to," I said, knowing she knew I knew nothing of the kind.

After another couple of minutes, she said, very quietly, "I'm actually a fairly dull person, you know. Without Milt, I wouldn't have any fun at all. A mother wants her family to be safe. But that's the thing about him. He never cared for a minute about being comfortable, let alone safe." She looked up at me. It was the oddest time for her to say "Jim, promise me, whatever happens you won't settle for just playing it safe?"

⁂

The storm was still raging all around the Bombshell. Inside the cockpit, Milt's face was white. He looked now more like a lost boy than a world-class explorer.

Odom was fighting from moment to moment to keep control of the plane.

Tex fiddled with the radio dial, but all he got was static.

Then one of the engines started to sputter.

"Starboard engine!" Tex called out.

"Can't run on fumes. Got to put her down," Odom grumbled.

"Where?" came the question from Milt.

"Pick your spot," Odom said. "It's a big ocean."

Not quite realizing the consequences, Milt wanted to know, "But where are we going to get fuel?"

"We're thumbing our next ride from the Coast Guard, Milt," Odom said, with surprising hopefulness.

"Where is the next airstrip?" he insisted on asking.

"Are you nuts?"

Tex studied his charts. "Adak Island," he replied. "Air Force cow path."

"We can gas up there," Milt said. "We're still ahead of the record."

Odom wasn't quite ready to say no. "Flight time?" he asked Sallee.

To come up with the answer, Tex had to recheck the instrument panel, look at his watch, and do the math quickly in his head. "Twelve minutes, give or take."

"Fuel?" Odom wanted all the data.

"It's close, Bill," Tex said. "No kidding, real close."

"Milt?" Amazingly, Odom wanted him to make the call.

As if to heighten the drama and give Milt his cue, lightning flashed again.

"I made a promise I intend to keep," he said.

℞

I thought the clock on the mantel was ticking so slowly it had stopped. The wait was as boring as it was excruciating. Mom had fallen asleep in her chair, and now Zelta was wide awake. She'd said she was going to read, but she couldn't manage it. I thought I could doze, but I couldn't.

The phone rang, and Mom's head jerked up. I managed to grab it before she did. If it was bad news, I wanted to be the one to take the blunt force of it and hopefully soften the blow to her.

It didn't take them long to tell me. This guy was remarkably terse. I guess he had other calls to make, like to all the news services. I thanked him and hung up the phone gently, thinking today was the first day of the rest of my life. I wasn't free, but I soon would be.

I'd thought about all the different ways it could go, what I would do. For sure, I didn't want him telling me what to do next. But then again, if he didn't make it through, the only baby Mom would have to coddle would be ours. Would she want to live with us? Would she come with us to California? Would she come and go from her own room as if she were some lodger? How long would that be possible before we couldn't stand each other anymore?

But if he did make it, what lunatic scheme would he want to drag me into next? And then, if his project wasn't right-out philanthropic, it would probably make a ton of money. Which would make it that much harder to turn it down or to leave.

The worst part of that kind of role would be the impossible errands. Which would have to be done right away, of course.

I couldn't stifle a yawn. I hoped it didn't seem disrespectful.

"Milt is giving out pens to the Air Force on some little island off Alaska," I said. I was already unbuttoning my shirt, on my way to the guest bedroom.

Mom squealed with delight, rushed over and hugged me. I kissed her back but kept moving.

I guess I'd sounded annoyed.

Zelta knew there was more. "So what's wrong?"

"He gave them instructions for me. He wants me to get him a meeting with the President of the United States."

ↄ

Later that day, the three of us boarded a train at Union Station, bound for Washington.

Meanwhile, the daring aviators were landing in New York, which established a new world's record for circumnavigating the globe by twin-engine aircraft—just short of seventy-nine hours, beating the Hughes record by a whopping twelve.

When they set the record by touching down at LaGuardia, Milt might have had visions of a ticker tape parade down Wall Street. But he was fixated on getting that meeting in the Oval Office. So they didn't waste any time. After a brief stopover, they continued on to National Airport in D.C.

21

We got our meeting at the White House. But I had nothing to do with it. Truman invited *him*.

So that's how I came to be standing on one foot and then the other at Winifred's desk, waiting for the big little guy to finish signing some bill. And by now you know why I prayed so fervently it wouldn't be with a ballpoint.

If you can believe it, Milt had been flirting with Winifred while I was in the can.

He was holding a copy of the *Washington Post* that had the picture of the flyers as the headline story on the front page.

I pointed to it as I walked past. "Fame. It's all about fame," I said, but not too loud.

Milt drew me aside to be sure she wouldn't overhear. "What's your point?"

Not answering him directly, I said, "Why do I have a bad feeling about this?"

Then his voice dropped to a whisper. "You know, she says he's got something for me."

"A lot of people do," I couldn't resist saying.

He wasn't about to be upset. Not today. I wondered if he thought I'd gotten him the meeting with the man from Missouri. I hadn't bothered to tell him one way or another. I figured, let him think I could do the impossible, this once.

"What do you think they do for this?" Milt wondered. "Congressional Medal of Honor?"

"You didn't exactly get wounded in action. And you didn't kill anybody. Did you?"

Winifred's intercom buzzed and she promptly announced, "Gentlemen, the President will see you now." No wink to Milt. She didn't even look up.

ᙣ

The room had been cleared from the signing ceremony. There must be a back way out. As we entered, the President stood up, something I didn't expect him to do. He came around his desk and shook our hands. He had a nice grin, something else I didn't expect. From the newsreels I thought he'd be something of a sourpuss.

And actually he was even shorter than I expected. But so was Napoleon, they say.

Right behind us came Tex and Odom. What, did they have trouble parking?

"This your crew?" the President asked Milt.

"Yessir," he said.

As he shook their hands, he muttered, "Fine job. 'Round the world. Show that smart-aleck Howard Hughes."

Grins all around. Apparently, Hughes' favorite sport was bullying politicians.

Milt couldn't wait for his medal.

Truman resumed his seat behind the desk (which was also smaller than I expected) and gestured for us to sit. We sat on guest chairs, not on the sofas. That should've told us something, I suppose.

The Leader of the Free World cleared his throat.

"Mr. Reynolds," he said somberly, "I've got something for you."

Wow, Winifred wasn't pulling his leg, after all. Milt was elated, over the Moon. He shot me a look and I knew he was thinking something like, "Notice it's not Odom. It's *me!*"

Truman reached into his desk drawer and pulled out an ordinary shoebox wrapped in plain brown paper.

He stared at it for a moment, as if unsure what the protocol should be.

He decided to stand, and so did we all.

Milton nudged the slightest bit forward. He wanted to be very sure Odom wouldn't grab the prize.

With a slow, ceremonial gesture but without grandiose pronouncement, Truman handed the box to Milt.

"May I?" Milt asked, forgetting to say thank you and wanting permission to tear into it.

"All yours," Truman said with his poker face.

As Milt unwrapped it, Truman turned to me and asked, "Know what I did before I was a judge?"

"You were a haberdasher, sir," I remembered.

Milt lifted the lid on the box to find it filled with ink-grimed pens.

"Yep," the President said. "Fred Gimbel is a friend of mine."

Odom leaned in to get a peek at Milt's prize and was bold enough to lift a gooey pen from the box.

He read the inscription, "I swiped this pen from Harry S. Truman."

As for the theft victim, he was not the least bit happy. "I guess people think I know how to get 'em fixed," he snapped.

A few minutes later, we were all in the Rose Garden posing for the press. Truman was grinning broadly as he shook hands with Odom, and Milt jostled me to make sure he was at least framed in the shot.

So Milt got his photo with Truman, but history records that the Commander-in-Chief shook hands with the pilot.

22

n the hospital waiting room, Milt and I were pacing in opposite directions.

In those days, they had to guess about a lot of things. They told us it would be a boy based on the heart rate the doctor had taken with his stethoscope listening through Zelta's swollen stomach.

And also back then, the men did not participate in or even attend the birth.

Later, Zelta told me that, as she pushed mightily to push the baby out, she said a few things about me she didn't mean.

I don't know where they'd taken the baby, but when they finally said I could see Zelta, she was lying in bed alone. She was soaked with sweat, and still pretty groggy.

A nurse came in after me holding an infant and saying, "A fine baby girl."

I informed her, "You must have the wrong room. We're having a boy."

She was really confused there for a moment, until Zelta snapped out of it and cried, "We'll take her!"

Our daughter, Jessie, would be the doctor in the family (seriously).

Of course, I was just as thrilled she was a she. But when we got home, Zelta did make a point of saying we could keep trying for a boy.

It's good to have a goal. And trying, in itself, has its own rewards.

∞

Zelta, Jessie, and I headed west to California, dusting off a plan we'd put on the shelf long enough for Milt to parlay his flying hobby into international headlines.

I took a job with an aircraft company. They called me a "sales engineer." I hated it.

My moods on returning home from work each day weren't the best. And to make matters worse, I was too proud to confess to Zelta that I wondered whether the move had been a mistake. I'd finally gotten what I wanted, after all. What was the use of complaining? I told myself maybe my attitude about the job would get better once I learned the ropes. But, day after day, it was mostly a lot of sales rejection, just the kind of challenge that fazed Milt not at all. It irritated me to think not only how bad I was at it, but also how much better he would have been peddling those aircraft parts, or anything.

Years later, as a student, Jessie showed signs of genuine mechanical aptitude. That's probably because Zelta saw no reason to invest in toys and let her play on the floor with the pots and pans. One day when I got home, her banging and clanging was particularly annoying. She was using a long-handled metal spoon to beat out a rhythm on a saucepan. My complaining about this triggered an argument, and for no particularly relevant reason, it came around to the subject of whether we should think about moving back.

My mother had fallen ill recently, and I'd been meaning to book a ticket to visit on one of my business trips back east.

So even though there were all kinds of reasons to go, I wasn't being decisive. "What about what's important to me?" Zelta demanded. "Or to us? I'd say it's family first, but you should already know that answer. Come to think of it, what's important to *you* these days?"

I walked away because I still didn't know what to say. Of course we should go. But I was still fretting about Milt and how I didn't want to show up on his doorstep with my hat in my hands.

Near me on the sideboard was a stack of mail. Zelta had brought it in, but she hadn't looked through it. So as she continued our "discussion," rudely I thumbed through it.

There was a letter addressed to me, not to us, in what I recognized as a shaky version of Edna's writing.

I ripped it open. She was writing from the hospital. I hadn't known. There had been no word of this, not at all. I thought it was some chronic kind of thing she had, and she was seeing somebody for it. But here's the rest, and the reason her note was intended just for me:

> *You were always worried about what your father wanted. Then you punched him and that settled that. Can't blame him for your choices anymore, can you? Remember, don't get too comfortable. Getting tired now. It hasn't exactly been a party around here.*

The tears came as I realized she was much worse off than I'd imagined. Perhaps she hadn't wanted to say. And certainly I should have asked.

I phoned Milt and didn't get much of an answer. Apparently he was in denial, too.

I traveled the next day, telling Zelta I'd send for them when I knew more.

I didn't get there in time.

∽

I switched jobs and we stayed in California, bought a house. It wasn't my dream job but it wasn't a chore, either. I tried to stay in touch with Milt, but Mom had always been the communicator when it came to family business. With him, it was all business. I'd send him baby news and snapshots, avoiding any mention of my work. And sometimes in reply I'd get a brief update on his personal letterhead, but sent from the office and all about his latest venture and plans. And getting him on the phone was next to impossible.

One day in 1952—seven years after that day we first wrote on a soggy newspaper—I received an engraved invitation from the Reynolds International Pen Company to a reception "In Honor of Our Chairman Milton Reynolds." There was no explanatory note as to the occasion or the reason for the party. As it turned out, I managed to think of a business reason to go back, and I decided I'd drop in. No prior arrangements, no fanfare. Beard the lion in his den. I figured, that way, if it was too awkward, I'd be able get out quickly without much fuss.

Awkward was hardly the word.

It was an evening function, involving a full banquet followed by an awards ceremony and dancing. I arrived hours late, as the dinner plates were being cleared, in the Grand Ballroom of the Palmer House. I flashed on Zelta and I dancing there at the end of the war. This time, the room was full of drunken people, but I didn't know many of them or the reason for their gaiety.

There was a dance-band orchestra on the dais. They started to play "For He's a Jolly Good Fellow." The crowd parted on the floor to make way for Milt, who was dancing a jig with the pen-tester twins, Marta and Magda. For his big finish, he bent Magda over for a prolonged Valentino-style kiss.

The crowd was wild for it.

I made my way over to the service bar. I needed a drink or three before I could deal with him.

But no sooner did I belly up than he danced over. His feigned drunkenness disappeared as he instructed the bartender, "Start watering the Scotch, and when you run out, give 'em tequila. After two drinks they won't know the difference."

Only then did he act as if he'd just seen me.

"Jim! Jim-boy!" Big, soulful embrace. Pat on the back.

"What's the big occasion?"

"Why, where have you been, on the planet Mars? We sold the pen company!"

I guess I didn't look all that happy. Should I have been consulted? Why? What did I expect? If he'd tried to give it to me, I'd probably have turned him down.

It was the end of an era, no question.

Before he went back to his guests, he put his hand on my arm and said, "She was a saint, your mother. Come on. Life belongs to the living."

I wouldn't talk to him for ten years after that.

∾

I never was much for religion. Milt was Jewish but never observant, and Edna never pushed her Christian Science on me. I was a Boy Scout, whose loyalties are supposed to be "For God and Country," which I suppose is more fervent than a lot of people ever get.

Years later, Milton had left this Earth but remained a frequent topic of conversation in the Reynolds clan. At those times, even the younger ones who knew him only by reputation learned to tell people he wasn't an *im*-moral man, just an *a*-moral one. And certainly, like some capitalist god, he really didn't factor right and wrong into his calculations. All he needed to decide was, "Will it be good for business?"

But I also judge Milt was essentially a Humanist, although he would not have known the term or owned up to it if he had. He believed in the power of a man (and if you pressed him, also a woman, if she so chose) to do anything he set his mind to. He believed in the force of will. And so many times, throughout the Pen Wars and everything that came afterward, Milt prevailed mainly because his will was stronger and more single-minded than that of his adversaries.

Just ask Martin Straus.

And, to wax even more philosophical, I'd say he was not alone in his outlook, which grew naturally from the collective experience of World War II. Back in the nineteenth century, the German thinker Friedrich Nietzsche had shocked the world by declaring, "God is dead." Meaning, I suppose, in view of both scientific observation and the undeniable presence of unbridled evil in the world—faith in a deity was no longer possible. He'd said this to a nation of Meistersingers, who prior to this time were poetry-loving Romantics, believing not only in God but also in the perfectibility of Man. A few generations later, along came the Nazis and decided, in effect, if there's no God, we'll have to take matters into our own hands. And in their efforts to engineer a master race, they ran roughshod over millions of people, including just about all of their neighbors. Now some of the patriots in the French Resistance didn't believe in God any more than the Nazis did. Partly in reaction to the horrors of war, thinkers like Albert Camus and Jean-Paul Sartre came to believe that the world, in fact the whole universe, is empty and meaningless. In the view of these Existentialists, there may be no right or wrong, but humans have a duty to each other to decide to act morally—because that's the only choice that works.

Many fathers, on all sides, resented their sons for not marching off to war, no matter what the reason. Their mothers secretly thanked God, even those to whom God was a stranger.

The American victors came to believe what Milt believed—they could achieve anything they set their minds to. But they also, most of them, had been taught to believe in some aspect of the Judeo-Christian God. So their answer was, "Let's figure out how to make a buck, and you can think what you want about God."

Or that was the idea for a while, anyway.

At some point, a man considers his mortality, and his options. My business would sometimes take me to downtown Los Angeles, where I always looked forward to having a traditional Mexican lunch on Oliveira Street. One day when

I was feeling particularly wistful, I decided to stop in at the old Our Lady Queen of the Angels church.

It was the middle of the afternoon on a weekday. I slid into a pew near the back. There was one older lady seated off to the side way in front. She had her head down the whole time.

I looked up at the image of the suffering Christ on the cross. Here was the son of God, wearing a crown of thorns, covered in Roman spit, his legs broken, and bleeding from a hole in his side.

And what was his big question, with his last breath? What was the one thing even he couldn't figure out?

"Father, why have you forsaken me?"

Maybe nobody gets it right.

∽

In the years after I left the pen company, Milt and I didn't communicate much at all. But I followed his exploits. He acquired another aircraft, a C-87 cargo plane, which he renamed the *China Explorer*. Again with Odom as well as a team of scientists, he'd gone off to prove the K2 peak in the Amne Machin mountain range bordering on China and Tibet was taller than Mt. Everest (which it isn't). But along the way he alienated the Red Chinese, who thought he was secretly looking for nuclear test sites. The Russians accused him of looking for evidence of uranium mines. And he made some friends in the U.S. government, who probably didn't mind if he'd just accidentally managed to get some happy snaps of any such places or activities.

However, I knew his real motivation when I learned that, had he been able to prove the maximal height of K2, he wanted it renamed Mount Reynolds.

He'd officially retired, but not before sensationalizing the pen business a few more times. Like the singer James Brown, his way of leaving the stage was to keep coming back for encores. Besides the original Reynolds pen that had sold more than any pen model in history, the Reynolds International Pen Company in just a few years had introduced the 400 (the pen that needs no cap), the Rocket and several spin-offs, including the Junior, Senior, and Super Rockets, as well as the Rocket Threesome (the Rockette and the Stubby Rocket sold in a set with the Rocket), and then the Bombshell and the Reynolds Flyer. (And I've probably missed a few.) At the end of this run, all of the major pen companies had their own models. Most of these were priced under a buck and cost about eight cents to make.

Milt sold the machine tooling for our pens to the Fisher Pen Company of Los Angeles. He sold the brand name to a French concern, which, in an irony lost on just about everybody, used it to market cheap, disposable *fountain pens* to schoolchildren who must learn cursive penmanship in elementary school. The Soviets started making ballpoints in Moscow at the Sacco & Vanzetti Pencil Factory (I swear, I'm not making that up). And, unbeknownst to me and just about everyone else involved with the company, he'd sold the corporate charter to the U.S. government. The CIA reportedly took control of it and renamed it the Reynolds Construction Company. From time to time (or so it was said), the espiocrats awarded contracts to this fictitious organization, through which they routed payments to political entities that Congress could not admit to dealing with, let alone pay.

Idi Amin may or may not have used some of this dough to buy a gold-plated Cadillac.

Milt's business colleagues denied these connections, and indeed it was likely that no one at Printasign even knew about them. These were, after all, separate companies. Also, his crew members on the expedition flatly denied any subterfuge. But the rumor persisted in the family that he was on some kind of spy mission.

I thought it was all bunk until a political journalist by the name of Alexander Cockburn described the clandestine-payment operation in a tell-all book. Very probably, few people inside the government knew why the project was code-named "KK Mountain," but, when I read this, several pieces of the puzzle clicked into place.

What Milt did next also fit the legend of amateur spy. Occasionally, he made the papers on his international travels, now as a commercial air passenger, but always flying first class. He'd drop in on some potentate or other. Who sent him and why were not mentioned in those publicity releases. By all reports, he was a "goodwill ambassador." He was just a crusty rich guy who loved the U S of A and wanted to bestow his largesse on starving populations.

Once he even tried to break the world's record for circumnavigating as a passenger on scheduled airlines and almost succeeded. Flying commercially, he booked six round-the-world trips in six years.

In the meantime, he'd retired to Mexico, where a well-to-do retired American could live like a king.

And he did. Word was, he'd shacked up with his house-keeper. Or was it her cousin? Or her daughter? Then, as if to compound the complications of his estate after his demise, he married one of them.

He bought a hacienda on a hillside outside Mexico City. It was so lavish, so grandiose, the family came to call it "the

Milton Hilton." Mind you, none of them had gone there yet. They just imagined.

So I decided I'd stop guessing and drop in on him.

The Jeep ride north from Mexico City over rough roads and up the mountainside could dislocate your kidneys. You had to *need* to go there.

I had a map and some general directions I'd gotten from what was left of his office in Chicago. He still retained a skeleton crew of PR flacks, and they were anxious to justify their salaries.

As I pulled into the circular drive, I could hear a long string of invectives coming from the house. In Spanish. She was very angry. Milton was making up for all manner of past sins, if he was the brunt of her anger.

If it were just he and the housekeeper up here, woe to both of them. Maybe they deserved each other. I didn't want to imagine.

He greeted me as if I'd seen him yesterday.

I accepted his offer of strong drink, and he escorted me through his palace, ending in a large study that housed his collection of wall-sized blow-up photos of himself on his worldwide exploits.

He excused the loud verbal ranting of his housemate. "Spirited woman" was all he said, and took a couple of gulps of his own drink, which I believe was straight tequila on ice, the kind they'd use for anesthetic if you were having an operation, like removing a bullet, and they didn't have anything else.

"Enjoying your retirement?" I asked.

"I don't get around much anymore," he said modestly, lying through his teeth.

We were looking at a huge four-by-eight photo of him on safari, one panel among many on a hinged wall display.

"Oh, yeah? I heard you were a messenger boy for the CIA." I couldn't resist.

"You mean that time with the Maharaja of Bundi?" That was the photo we were looking at. "Some big game there, I can tell you." This was a story he could talk about.

"No business deals?" I asked. I knew there were some. There had to be.

"You're talking about the Big Idea?" He was so damn coy. Here he was, at an age when his peers would have hung it up, thrown in the towel, and he was still pulling strings. And, worse, lying about it to me, who knew better.

He sat me down and freshened my drink from his bottle. Then his voice grew hushed.

"Little company in Panama—Syntex. They came up with this pill. A woman takes it, see, as a precaution."

Where was he going with this? What cockamamie idea was he chasing now?

"It's this pill," he explained. "A birth. Control. Pill."

I took a gulp of my drink. I could only begin to imagine how disruptive such an invention could be. Women in control of whether they gave birth? Rubbers were one thing, a precaution you had to put on, struggle with, and pray didn't break. Now, I can tell you, truth be told, it's not at all about breaking. Men are all cowards to admit, when their equipment contracts after it's over, the infernal thing doesn't break—it *slips off!* But who is going to admit their member got so tiny and they were so lame as to *leave it behind* in their partner? No, the thing *broke!* It was not *big enough* for my manhood!

Anyhow, Milt had shaken up the world with the pen. Now he was going straight at the gonads. Had he no shame?

I didn't want in. I didn't want anywhere near it. Not on moral grounds, but because I couldn't imagine the risks or the mitigations. I was investment shy. I shouldn't have been, but that was the difference between him and me.

He was also partners with investor Charlie Allen, buying up real estate in what would become the suburbs of Mexico City.

Oh, and they'd sunk money into Iranian oil. Don't get me started.

Anyhow, I told him I didn't want into any of his schemes. "I'll pass," I said. "But I do want to buy what's left of the old company—not the pens."

"You want to sell printing equipment to cheapskate retailers? You can have it."

Yes, I did. I did very much. Printasign was a solid enterprise, one that had lasted for decades, and I figured with my engineering background and what little sales expertise I'd gotten from him, I could grow the business.

Then and there, we agreed. I could have it for a dollar and a percentage of the profits for a period of time. It was the best deal I ever made. And best of all, I could call it mine, and whatever happened, good or bad, it would be my responsibility. If it failed, I would not be able to cop out by blaming him. And if it succeeded, well, that would be sweet.

As I drove away, I could hear her cursing at him to the sound of smashing crockery.

Excitement gravitated to him, and he was never shy.

∽

It was some years later. Printasign was still a going concern, and I'd found a business to run I didn't half mind. In fact, it was a pleasure. It was the same old gang of money-grinding retailers I'd known from the pen days. But it was honor among thieves. No, not thieves, sharp-dealing business-people who didn't give an inch.

Here I was sitting on the dais at the Continental Hotel in Century City. I was the guest of honor—can you imagine?

That night, I accepted my award from the gracious hands of the man I'd sold to, cheated, and befriended— Fred Gimbel.

"National Retail Federation Businessman of the Year. Congratulations, Jim." Gimbel, always the gracious host, handed me my gleaming statuette.

As I stepped up to the podium, I said, "Some of you won't remember that the Reynolds Pen Company made the first ballpoint pens, which leaked."

Polite titters of laughter from the audience.

"I guess we did a lot for the garment business."

Bigger laughs.

"Since then," I went on, "we've made a few honest dollars."

I went on from there, but it was the usual self-promotional bull. I owed a lot of it to Milt, much as I tried to push the thought from my mind that night.

છ

After the banquet, having kicked off our shoes at home in our bedroom, Zelta and I danced in our trademark close, sexy, dreamy embrace. The vertical expression of a horizontal desire. The song on the hi-fi was Benny Goodman's "Moonlight Serenade."

Zelta loosened my bow tie. "I get to sleep with the businessman of the year."

"Who says you get to sleep?"

"Well, okay," she said coyly. "Let's just don't wake the kids." Yeah, we'd tried and tried. And been blessed with more.

"Did we settle for comfortable?" I asked. I was half serious, because tonight it seemed, yes we had.

"Are you kidding?" she shot back. "All those times we thought we couldn't make payroll? And then that airhead little bookkeeper—"

Uh-oh. I didn't need to be reminded about *her*. The train wreck that almost happened. "Okay, okay," I said.

"I'm going to have a love affair with a movie producer," she announced, ever so lightly, as if it were her turn.

"Oh, yeah?" Now I was afraid of the answer.

"Some guy called today, asked for you. Wants to make a picture about Milt."

"The pen story?"

"The daring aviator."

"Hoo boy."

"I told him," she said. "Ridiculous."

"Oh, yeah," I agreed. "Ridiculous."

Then it occurred to me. "It has to be a musical!"

⁊

Why did I say it had to be a musical?

It just seemed there was no better way to capture the essential Milton. You had to laugh—there was no other way to take him.

And I realized, so much later, after he was gone, that having a rocket in your pocket is something every man can understand. It's why you get up every morning. It's the insane hope that lights you up and keeps you on the quest, whether you are peddling jet engines or printing equipment or video lighters. It's the sizzle of the pitch, the satisfaction of the sale, and—let's be honest—the perennial hope you'll finally get lucky with your favorite girl.

Women—I don't know what gets them going, and I never will. God love 'em.

But fathers and sons, they do the crazy dance.

⁊

INT. BROADWAY STAGE - FANTASY - NIGHT

Jim and Milt SING and dance a duet to the SWING TUNE
of the '40s version of "The Rocket Song."

JIM AND MILT

[shout] It's the Rocket! Rocket!

[sing] What's all the talk about the latest pen that's out?

It's the Rocket. I mean, the Rocket.

Every Jill and Joe who's really in the know,

They've got a Rocket. In their pocket.

Even Mom and Dad, they put a Rocket

In Little Junior's jumper pocket.

Have a look around, the world is Rocket-bound.

They all envy me.

Got a Rocket in my pocket. I'm walking on air.

With a Rocket in my pocket I can write 'most anywhere—

In any lane, up in the sky, or deep down in the sea.

It writes too high, for years and years.

Sensational, you'll agree.

Got a Rocket in my pocket, my future looks bright.

I'm so happy with my Rocket, I'm writin' all right.

To be specific, it's terrific—ahead of them all.

Just a flick and a click [click! click!]

And you write on the ball!

With the rocket in your pocket, you're ahead of them all.
Just a flick and a click [click! click!]
And you write on the ball!
[kazoo! shout] Rocket!

The number segues to a wild ROCK 'N ROLL VERSION as they dance into the wings and just as quickly dance back on—with Jim-as-Elvis on lead guitar and Milt doing a duck-walk with a funky bass.

More cast members dance onto the stage, as the scene builds to a boffo production number. Big Reynolds Rockets are wheeled on, accompanied by Marta and Magda in drum-majorette dress.

Sailing above them on wires, Gimbel and Straus fly in on matching miniature biplanes.

It's a sensational curtain-call finish as they belt out a NEW CHORUS:

ALL SING to JIM'S LEAD VOCAL

Got a Rocket in my pocket,
And I'm ready to roll.
Got a Rocket in my pocket,
And the Moon is my goal!

Got a Rocket in my pocket,
So get ready to squeal.
Got a Rocket in my pocket—
It's the best way to feel.

Got a Rocket in my pocket—
Come on, Baby, let's split.
Got a Rocket in my pocket,
And my thrusters are lit!

ROLL CREDITS over a montage of outtakes from the "Messy Period" and "Law of Gravity" scenes.

FADE OUT.

Afterword

Jim's first-person narrative may give the reader the impression that this work of fiction was somehow adapted from his memoirs. But although there is a wealth of Reynolds ephemera, no such personal document exists. The historian in me (the author speaking now) needs to confess that my creative self has taken considerable liberties with the truth. The surprising revelation will be that the bizarre, madcap, and often questionable schemes of Milton Reynolds, as recounted in this story, actually happened much as I have described them. As to Milt's character or his actions, there was no need to invent or exaggerate. It's the more mundane stuff that I had to make up. In particular, Jim's role in the development and marketing of the Reynolds ballpoint is deliberately overstated here. Although Milton orchestrated, choreographed, and conducted all of his company's antics in the Pen Wars, he had not just Jim but a coterie of advisors and collaborators supporting him. Among these were marketing genius and pen-company president Franklin Lamb, legal counsel Julian Levi, sales executive Stanley Schary (brother of Hollywood mogul Dore), advertising counsel Dave Wolff (who claimed to have discovered Jack Benny), and financial advisor Paul Levy, along with a corps of mechanical engineers and expert machinists, including William Huenergardt, Titus Haffa, Sig H. Hagen, and Ed Heil. A lone counterbalance for all these men was Milton's wife Edna, who was a potent force in his multiple business ventures, as well as his faithful companion on many globetrotting sales trips.

So, for storytelling purposes, the contributions of these people toward the success (or lack of it) of the Reynolds Pen are consolidated in the fictional character of Jim. But the strength of character, wry humor, and wisdom of the historical James Reynolds were, if anything, more impressive than I've portrayed him. And perhaps most important, his relationship with his boisterous father was pretty much as described. Huckster extraordinaire Milton was prone to fits of temper, exaggeration, and overpromising. His quiet son Jim was understated, cool under fire, and scrupulously honest. To me, the engine of comedy between these two personality types was irresistible, and it's the true-to-life heart of the ballpoint story.

Jim did in fact graduate from Stanford with an engineering degree, and he did marry the campus catch, Zelta Burrows. I didn't need to embellish her fierce independence, sharp wit, or canny mistrust of Milton. But Jim's actual role in the pen game is somewhat open to question. It may well be that some of the innovations I have attributed to him originated in his quiet suggestions. He was that modest, and Milt was that overbearing, particularly as concerned a stubbornly truthful son who had a lot to learn about being a salesman.

Around the time Milton cashed out of the pen business, he allowed his son to purchase the predecessor company Reynolds Printasign, which Jim ran capably—excelling in both manufacturing savvy as well as salesmanship—until his death in 1988. I'd met Jim just two months before his passing. A mutual friend, consulting engineer John Cool, referred me to write a series of magazine articles on the history of the company. I interviewed Jim and his son Tom, who at the time was national sales manager of Printasign. Of course, they couldn't resist telling this news junkie about the Pen Wars, Milton's record-breaking flight around the world in his twin-engine Douglas A-26, and his air expedition to establish the height of the K2 mountain range in Tibet. During our conversation, I couldn't help thinking this Milton Reynolds was some kind of real-world Indiana Jones. When I shared with them that I thought the story would make a great action-adventure movie, Jim chuckled and said quietly, "It should be a musical."

I thought his comment odd at the time, but of course now that you know the story, we both understand exactly what he meant.

The facts of the ballpoint story and Milt's subsequent exploits are mostly in the public record. I've included my principal sources in the references appended to this book. Of these, most notable are Thomas Whiteside's coverage of the Pen Wars in *The New Yorker* and Robert L. Rosenberg's comprehensive and meticulously researched doctoral thesis on the life and career of Milton Reynolds. I had the privilege of working for Reynolds Printasign and its successor company The Reynolds Group for ten years, and in some respects you could say once assigned the role of company historian, I wasn't about to give it up. I'm particularly grateful to Henry Gostony, contributing editor of *Pen World*, who interviewed me for a series of articles in that magazine. Henry's interest in the various Reynolds ballpoint models ended up infecting a whole new generation of pen collectors, along with some colorful older types who still covet "the pen that writes under water." (If you happen to find one that's still working, don't write me—alert the media!)

My first fictional adaptation of the ballpoint story took the form of a script for a feature film. That script won a Screenwriters Laboratory award from The Independent Feature Project West, the indie filmmakers' group now known as Film Independent. In the lab over the course of a summer, I refined the story under the direction of Josh Welsh where I was mentored by Lee David Zlotoff, whom I credit with the suggestion to begin the action outside the Oval Office.

Over the years, Tom Reynolds has been a boss, mentor, colleague, and friend. He and his wife Meredith have consistently encouraged me, even as my storytelling delved perilously into sensitive areas of their family history. And from time to time, Tom invited me to lunch with Zelta, even as her health began to fail, and those are among my fondest memories. Tom's three sisters have also been supportive—Jessie the medical researcher, Paula the philanthropist, and Mandy the drama coach. When I was struggling with the script, I wanted to make sure that Zelta would approve. But much as Tom and I encouraged her, the alien script format was too daunting and her attention lapsed as she tried to read. So with Mandy's help and a hand from my friend film director Bruce Logan, we put on a staged reading of the script in the Keck Theatre of Occidental College. Tom made sure Zelta had a front-row seat, and he made it almost mandatory attendance for Printasign employees and their families. When the young actor who was to play Jim didn't show up on time, Zelta looked over at me with a tear in her eye and said, "You should play him." I choked up as a lump came to my throat. Fortunately, the world was spared my Los Angeles stage debut as the wayward actor finally appeared in the wings, and then it was on with the show. Somebody gave Zelta roses.

My own creative team deserves profuse thanks, including copyeditor Thomas Page, book and cover designer Gary Palmatier, rights editor Lewis W. O'Brien, and publicists Jason Teahan, AnaLise Matheson, and Robin Bridge. Throughout both the script and the book projects, my long-time entertainment attorney and steadfast friend Jay Kenoff has helped guide my steps. And my wife Georja Umano Jones, whose energy and enthusiasm seem boundless, inspires me every day.

Short-lived and unreliable as it eventually proved to be, the Reynolds ballpoint was a milestone not only in the technology of paperwork production but also in postwar consumer marketing. So, in a sense we have Milton Reynolds to thank for the necessity of at least two enduring government initiatives—the Paperwork Reduction Act and the Bureau of Consumer Protection.

Gerald Everett Jones
Santa Monica, Calif., June 2014

Selected References

Acker, Bill, "Reynolds Pen Company," *Bill's Pens*. http://www
.billspens.com/billspens/reynolds/reynolds.htm.

"After Ball Points, What?" *The New Yorker*, April 12, 1952, pp.
25–26. Follow-up article on Milton Reynolds' retirement.

Ament, Phil, "Ballpoint Pen: Fascinating Facts About the Invention," *The Great Idea Finder*, May 5, 2006. http://www.idea
finder.com/history/inventions/ballpen.htm.

"The Ballpoint Pen," *Quido Magazine Q-Klub*. http://www.quido
.cz/objevy/propis.a.htm.

Brannon, W. T., *The Milton Reynolds China Expedition*, Reynolds
Printasign Co., 1948. I believe the Brannon article appeared
originally in a pulp magazine, then the company reprinted it
as a publicity piece, along with news clips about the expedition. Brannon, who died in 1981, was also biographer of
confessed master con-man J.R. "Yellow Kid" Weil.

Cockburn, Leslie and Alexander Cockburn, "The CIA Paid Its Israeli Spies With Money From 'Under the Mattress,'" *Los Angeles Times*, September 1, 1991. This article is a brief summary of the book cited below.

Cockburn, Leslie and Alexander Cockburn, *Dangerous Liaison: The Inside Story of the U.S.-Israeli Covert Relationship*, Harper Perennial (1992), p. 101. Cited page has the reference to the Reynolds corporate charter reportedly used in the KK Mountain operation.

Derby, George and James Terry White (eds.), "Reynolds, Milton," *National Cyclopedia of American Biography*, Vol. 59, pp. 184–185.

Derby, George and James Terry White (eds.), "Straus, Martin Louis II," *National Cyclopedia of American Biography*, Vol. 48, pp. 17–18.

"Double-Barreled Feat," *Time*, April 28, 1947, pp. 85–86.

Ericson, Robert, "Engineering the Ball Point," *Pen World*, Fall 1989, pp. 27, 30–31, 38, 40–41, 44. Includes not only pictures of various pens but also technical explanations of their mechanisms.

"Fountain-Pen Scramble," *Fortune*, July 1946, p. 144. Contemporaneous coverage of the Pen Wars.

"The Function of Mountains," *Time*, April 12, 1948, p. 41. Amne Machin expedition.

G. M. Pens International, Pvt. Ltd. is the exclusive licensee of Reynolds Pens (France) [later acquired by Sanford Corporation] in India and the SAARC countries. Corporate website: http://reynolds-india.com/reynolds/corporate.

Gostony, Henry, "The Reynolds Ballpoint," *Pen World*, Vol. 7, No. 6 (July/August 1994), pp. 16, 18–19, 56.

Gostony, Henry, "Reynolds—Part II," *Pen World*, Vol. 8, No. 1 (September/October 1994), pp. 18, 20, 52–53, 60.

Gostony, Henry, "Milton Reynolds: Part III," *Pen World*, Vol. 8, No. 2 (November/December 1994), pp. 34–35, 59, 64.

Gostony, Henry and Stuart L. Schneider. *The Incredible Ball Point Pen: A Comprehensive History and Price Guide (A Schiffer Book for Collectors)*, Schiffer Pub Ltd (1998). The historical material in this book mostly recaps the *Pen World* articles cited above but also has market specifics on the collectibles.

Green, Daniel S., "Jack Owens: The Cruising Crooner," "Jack Owens: Discography," and "Jack Owens: Official Myspace Page," *The Peanut Gallery* website www.rogerowenspeanut man.com. Best source of information I found on "The Rocket Song" and its singer-songwriter, who was a frequent performer on "Don McNeill's Breakfast Club" radio (and later TV) show. A subsequent 1950s song "I've Got a Rocket in My Pocket," attributed to Lowell George, has the same (alternate) title but is apparently an entirely different work, not the tune or the lyrics commissioned by Reynolds in 1946. "The Rocket Song" was published on the flip side of Owens' hit tune, "How Soon (Will I Be Seeing You?)."

"Guaranteed to Write 2 Years Without Refilling," *New York Times,* October 28, 1945. Gimbels' display ad for premiere of the Reynolds Pen the following day at the Manhattan store.

Herman, Charlotte and Helen Cogancherry (ill.), *Millie Cooper, 3B,* E. P. Dutton (1985). This children's book is written as a fictional memoir by the title character, a schoolgirl in 1946 Chicago. Her fondest wish is for a new Reynolds Rocket ballpoint so her written assignments for school won't have inkblots from her leaky fountain pen. She eventually gets one. It not only leaks but also skips and then won't write at all. Writing decades after the demise of the Reynolds pen enterprise, author Herman apparently relied on her own childhood memories. The details she includes about the pen are accurate, such as the choice of colors for the aluminum pen barrel and the ink.

"Hotter Than Ever," *Time,* February 24, 1947, pp. 89–90. Pen Wars follow-up on the *Time* November 12, 1945 article.

"Jones, Gerald E. and Thomas B. Reynolds, "The Launch and Rapid Return to Earth of the Reynolds Rocket," Los Angeles Pen Show Keynote, Radisson Hotel, Manhattan Beach, Calif., February 12, 1994.

Kyatang, Woo, "A Ballpoint Pen Man Views Immortality," *Shanghai Evening Post,* March 26, 1948. Milton anticipates the K2 peak's being named after him.

Lamb, Franklin, et al, *Write on the Ball,* Reynolds International Pen Company brochure, circa 1950.

"Milton Reynolds Papers," *Manuscript Collection No. 1240 (circa 1936–1987)*, University Libraries, University of Washington.

"Milton Reynolds, Pen Maker, Dead; Popularized the Ballpoint Pen—Set a Flight Speed Mark," *New York Times* obituary, January 25, 1976, p. 45.

"Miracle Pen," *Fortune*, August 1945, pp. 216, 219.

"Notes and Comment: Talk of the Town," *The New Yorker*, February 23, 1946. Follow-up story on the Thomas Whiteside feature article.

"On the Ball," *Time*, April 22, 1946, p. 82. Initial profitability of the Reynolds International Pen Co., along with challenges and potential competition.

"Pen Phenomenon," *Business Week*, December 15, 1945, pp. 84, 86.

"Penman in Tokyo," *Life*, April 28, 1947, pp. 47–48.

"Peripatetic Penman," *Newsweek*, April 19, 1948, pp. 70–71. The photo caption on Milt admiring a globe reads, "Reynolds: One trip too many."

"Pointless Pen," *Time*, August 21, 1944, p. 62. Tells of Biro's ball-bearing Stratopen, which preceded the first Reynolds model. The name derives from its use at high altitude by the Royal Air Force to keep flight logs.

"Reynolds Issue," *Business Week*, June 15, 1946, pp. 44–45. Stock market news: "Ball bearing pen concern plans to offer

100,000 shares to public and 'insiders' will sell an additional 300,000."

Reynolds, Milton, *Hasta La Vista (I'll Be Seeing You)*, Greenberg Publisher (1944). A collection of Milton's letters written while on sales trips abroad for Printasign, mostly to Central and South America. Introduction by Franklin Lamb (company president) and sketches by Josie St. Hill. These adventures predate the ballpoint story. Milt had his own plane at the time, the Stinson mentioned herein and dubbed *The Flying Printasign*, piloted by Roger Q. Williams, reportedly the first person to fly from New York to Rome.

"Reynolds Pen Files Million Suit," *New York Times*, October 7, 1945, Business & Finance, p. F5.

"Reynolds Plans New Round-World Flight," *Aviation Week*, July 7, 1947, p. 13. Description hints the goal might have been more than just measuring altitude: "Scientific data are to be obtained by ten technical experts expected to comprise crew and passengers on the new flight. Data will be made available to government and civilian scientific agencies, who will loan equipment for the journey." As Jim reports accurately in his fictional narrative, the Boston Science Museum helped fund the flight.

Rosenberg, Robert L., "Qum-1956: A Misadventure in Iranian Oil," *The Business History Review*, Vol. 49, No. 1 (Spring, 1975), pp. 81–104. Describes one of Milt's business ventures after his retirement to his hacienda in the hills above Mexico City.

Rosenberg, Robert L., *The Ventures and Adventures of an Errant Entrepreneur: Milton (Ball-Point) Reynolds (1892–1976),* University of Washington (1971). Ph.D. thesis. Several sources, including Whiteside, state Reynolds discovered the pen on a trip to Argentina. Rosenberg, however, maintains that Louis Goldblatt showed Reynolds the pen, then Milt went looking for its inventor. This is the version Jim tells in this story. As to surreptitious motives for the Amne Machin expedition, on p. 131 Rosenberg states that, prior to the Reynolds Bombshell round-the-world flight, Reynolds met with Lt. Gen. William Kepner in Honolulu. The military man was said to be curious about the feasibility of placing a nuclear detection post in the area Reynolds intended to explore. Rosenberg adds there was no further evidence Reynolds ever acted on this direction or reported back. Oral history in the family is that Milt was on some sort of secret mission, but there are no specifics.

"Science: There She Stands," *Time,* April 26, 1948. Addresses question of whether Amne Machin is world's highest peak, mentions Reynolds.

Taugher, Tim, "Brea, OH Plane Crash, September 1949," Bill Odom obituary, *GenDisasters,* Nov. 29, 2008. http://www3 .gendisasters.com/ohio/10112/berea-oh-plane-crash-sept-1949.

"Tempest in an Inkpot," *Time,* November 12, 1945, p. 84. Describes series of lawsuits filed in the Pen Wars.

Wharton, Don, "Mighty Battle of the Pens," *Nation's Business,* November, 1946, pp. 53–54, 98, 100. Another comprehensive feature article that helps round out Rosenberg and Whiteside.

Whiteside, Thomas, "Where Are They Now? The Amphibious Pen," *The New Yorker* (February 17, 1951), pp. 39–69. Besides Rosenberg, the best survey of the ballpoint story.

Georja Umano

Gerald Everett Jones is a freelance writer who lives in Santa Monica, California, with his wife—actress-comedienne, writer, and animal activist Georja Umano—and two Jack Russell Terrorists, Roxie and Romeo. His first book under the LaPuerta imprint was *How to Lie with Charts*. He expounds on his notions of male-centered humor in his collection of short stories, *Boychik Lit*, which includes an essay on the genre. He authored the boychik-lit series of Rollo Hemphill's comic misadventures: *My Inflatable Friend, Rubber Babes,* and *Farnsworth's Revenge.* Jones is a member of the Writers Guild of America, the Dramatists Guild, and Film Independent (FIND), as well as a past director of the Independent Writers of Southern California (IWOSC). He holds a Bachelor of Arts with Honors from the

College of Letters, Wesleyan University, where he studied under novelists Peter Boynton *(Stone Island)*, F.D. Reeve *(The Red Machines)*, and Jerzy Kozinski *(The Painted Bird, Being There)*. He blogs about male-centered comic fiction at www.boychiklit.com.

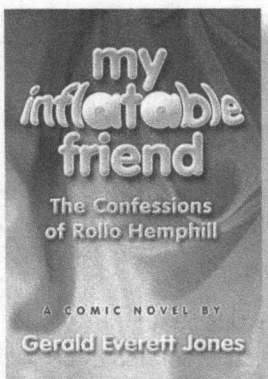

My Inflatable Friend

ISBN: 978-0-9794866-1-6 paper; 978-0-9794866-0-9 Kindle

To make his girlfriend jealous, Rollo dresses a life-sized rubber doll to look like glamorous Hollywood star Monica LaMonica, then drives it around town. When tabloids confront the real actress about her new affair, she confesses for reasons of her own, and Rollo gets much more than he bargained for.

Rubber Babes

ISBN: 978-0-9794856-4-7 paper; 978-0-9794866-3-0 Kindle

Settling down for a life in the happily-ever-after, Rollo thinks he's landed a cushy job heading up a Hollywood charity. Then he realizes too late it's a money laundry for an international criminal conspiracy—and he's being set up to take the rap when the Feds come calling.

Farnsworth's Revenge

ISBN: 978-0-9856227-2-5 paper; 978-0-9856227-3-2 Kindle

Rubber-Monica has disappeared from crusty Hugo Farnsworth's yacht in St. Tropez. Rollo gets drafted as an unofficial government operative to deal with the kidnappers. The doll has become a pawn in plot hatched by an eccentric Turk who collects lookalikes—and state secrets, including the plans for cold fusion and a scheme for bankrupting the world's money supply.

*by **Gerald Everett Jones***

Christmas Karma

ISBN: 978-09856227-6-3 trade paperback;
978-0-9856227-7-0 Kindle

Humorous Fiction (ages 14 and up)

C**hristmas Karma is a touching and witty tale** about the travails of a dysfunctional family around the holidays, narrated by an angel who has a wicked sense of humor. Main character Willa Nawicki is bewildered by a series of curious karmic events that literally ring her doorbell during the frantic season, awakening years-old resentments and stimulating ever-more-intense personal confrontations. These bizarre visitations include a grizzled old man claiming to be her father, who has been missing for some thirty years but now says the title to the family home is in his name – and now he wants the place back.

As the angel observes, "The surest way to invoke the laughter of the universe is to make plans, particularly devious ones."

The author says: "I wrote Christmas Karma after I'd gone through a series of personal losses. You don't need to have any particular brand of religious faith—or any at all—to enjoy this book. Most of all, please don't take any of it too seriously. May it bring you some welcome tears and laughter."

"This homage to Anne Tyler is a Christmas parable for the rest of us—whether faithful, backsliders, slackers, or just I-don't-knowists."

—**Thomas Page**, author of
The Man Who Would Not Die

"A funny, charming and unexpected tale of holiday dysfunction at its best. A Christmas treat all wrapped up in cactus, Southern California style. You never know who will ring the doorbell next at Willa's house, but you know they bring a touch of magic."

—**Lian Dolan**, bestseller author of *Helen of Pasadena*

"Of the many inquiries we get, this has been the most interesting in a long time."

—**The Very Rev. Harry E. Krauss** (retired)

"Alva Vanderbilt Belmont would be very grateful to you for researching a Vanderbilt family painting—as will all the family. And as I do. Historians keep us alive!"

—**Margaret Hayden Rector,** Vanderbilt biographer, author of *Alva, That Vanderbilt-Belmont Woman*

"I think you've done an extraordinary job of researching and speculating on the painting. You've certainly convinced me that this was a Vanderbilt affair!"

—**Mary Sudman Donovan,** Historian, Episcopal Church USA, Author of *A Different Call: Women's Ministries in the Episcopal Church, 1850–1920*